The Valley of Spiders

The Story of the Late Mr. Elvesham

I said, " How the devil did I get here? . . ."
and the voice was not my own.

It was not my own, it was thin, the
articulation was slurred, the resonance of
my facial bones was different. Then to
reassure myself I ran one hand over the
other, and felt loose folds of skin, the bony
laxity of age. Almost as quickly as if I did
it involuntarily, I thrust my fingers into my
mouth. My teeth had gone. My finger-tips
ran on the flaccid surface of an even row
of shrivelled gums. I was sick with dismay
and disgust.

**Available in Fontana
by the same author**

Love and Mr. Lewisham
The Invisible Man
Kipps

The Valley of Spiders

Short Stories by
H. G. Wells

Fontana / Collins

This selection first issued in Fontana Books
  1964
Second Impression August 1965
Third Impression September 1972
Fourth Impression May 1974

Printed in Great Britain
Collins Clear-Type Press
London and Glasgow

CONTENTS

POLLOCK AND THE PORROH MAN

IT was in a swampy village on the lagoon river behind the Turner Peninsula that Pollock's first encounter with the Porroh man occurred. The women of that country are famous for their good looks—they are Gallinas with a dash of European blood that dates from the days of Vasco de Gama and the English slave-traders, and the Porroh man, too, was possibly inspired by a faint Caucasian taint in his composition. (It's a curious thing to think that some of us may have distant cousins eating men on Sherboro Island or raiding with the Sofas.) At any rate, the Porroh man stabbed the woman to the heart as though he had been a mere low-class Italian, and very narrowly missed Pollock. But Pollock, using his revolver to parry the lightning stab which was aimed at his deltoid muscle, sent the iron dagger flying, and, firing, hit the man in the hand.

He fired again and missed, knocking a sudden window out of the wall of the hut. The Porroh man stooped in the doorway, glancing under his arm at Pollock. Pollock caught a glimpse of his inverted face in the sunlight, and then the Englishman was alone, sick and trembling with the excitement of the affair, in the twilight of the place. It had all happened in less time than it takes to read about it.

The woman was quite dead, and having ascertained this, Pollock went to the entrance of the hut and looked out. Things outside were dazzling bright. Half a dozen of the porters of the expedition were standing up in a group near the green huts they occupied, and staring towards him, wondering what the shots might signify. Behind the little group of men was the broad stretch of black fetid mud by the river, a green carpet of rafts and papyrus and water-grass, and then the leaden water. The mangroves beyond the stream loomed indistinctly through the blue haze. There were no signs of excitement in the squat village, whose fence was just visible above the cane-grass.

Pollock came out of the hut cautiously and walked towards the river, looking over his shoulder at intervals. But the Porroh man had vanished. Pollock clutched his revolver nervously in his hand.

One of his men came to meet him, and as he came, pointed to the bushes behind the hut in which the Porroh man had disappeared. Pollock had an irritating persuasion of having made an absolute fool of himself; he felt bitter, savage, at the turn things had taken. At the same time, he would have to tell Waterhouse— the moral, exemplary, cautious Waterhouse—who would inevitably take the matter seriously. Pollock cursed bitterly at his luck, at Waterhouse, and especially at the West Coast of Africa. He felt consummately sick of the expedition. And in the back of his mind all the time was a speculative doubt where precisely within the visible horizon the Porroh man might be.

It is perhaps rather shocking, but he was not at all upset by the murder that had just happened. He had seen so much brutality during the last three months, so many dead women, burnt huts, drying skeletons, up the Kittam River in the wake of the Sofa cavalry, that his senses were blunted. What disturbed him was the persuasion that this business was only beginning.

He swore savagely at the black, who ventured to ask a question, and went on into the tent under the orange-trees where Waterhouse was lying, feeling exasperatingly like a boy going into the head master's study.

Waterhouse was still sleeping off the effects of his last dose of chlorodyne, and Pollock sat down on a

8

packing-case beside him, and, lighting his pipe, waited for him to awake. About him were scattered the pots and weapons Waterhouse had collected from the Mendi people, and which he had been repacking for the canoe voyage to Sulyma.

Presently Waterhouse woke up, and after judicial stretching, decided he was all right again. Pollock got him some tea. Over the tea the incidents of the afternoon were described by Pollock, after some preliminary beating about the bush. Waterhouse took the matter even more seriously than Pollock had anticipated. He did not simply disapprove, he scolded, he insulted.

"You're one of those infernal fools who think a black man isn't a human being," he said. "I can't be ill a day without you must get into some dirty scrape or other. This is the third time in a month that you have come crossways-on with a native, and this time you're in for it with a vengeance. Porroh, too! They're down upon you enough as it is, about that idol you wrote your silly name on. And they're the most vindictive devils on earth! You make a man ashamed of civilisation. To think you come of a decent family! If ever I cumber myself up with a vicious, stupid young lout like you again——"

"Steady on, now," snarled Pollock, in the tone that always exasperated Waterhouse; "steady on."

At that Waterhouse became speechless. He jumped to his feet. "Look here, Pollock," he said, after a struggle to control his breath. "You must go home. I won't have you any longer. I'm ill enough as it is through you——"

"Keep your hair on," said Pollock, staring in front of him. "I'm ready enough to go."

Waterhouse became calmer again. He sat down on the camp-stool. "Very well," he said. "I don't want a row, Pollock, you know, but it's confoundedly annoying to have one's plans put out by this kind of thing. I'll come to Sulyma with you and see you safe aboard——"

"You needn't," said Pollock. "I can go alone. From here."

"Not far," said Waterhouse. "You don't understand this Porroh business."

"How should *I* know she belonged to a Porroh man?" said Pollock bitterly.

"Well, she did," said Waterhouse; "and you can't undo the thing. Go alone, indeed! I wonder what they'd do to you. You don't seem to understand that this Porroh hokey-pokey rules this country, is its law, religion, constitution, medicine, magic. . . . They appoint the chiefs. The Inquisition, at its best, couldn't hold a candle to these chaps. He will probably set Awajale, the chief here, on to us. It's lucky our porters are Mendis. We shall have to shift this little settlement of ours. . . . Confound you, Pollock! And, of course, you must go and miss him."

He thought, and his thoughts seemed disagreeable. Presently he stood up and took his rifle. "I'd keep close for a bit, if I were you," he said, over his shoulder, as he went out. "I'm going out to see what I can find out about it."

Pollock remained sitting in the tent, meditating. "I was meant for a civilised life," he said to himself, regretfully, as he filled his pipe. "The sooner I get back to London or Paris the better for me."

His eye fell on the sealed case in which Waterhouse had put the featherless poisoned arrows they had bought in the Mendi country. "I wish I had hit the beggar somewhere vital," said Pollock viciously.

Waterhouse came back after a long interval. He was not communicative, though Pollock asked him questions enough. The Porroh man, it seems, was a prominent member of that mystical society. The village was interested, but not threatening. No doubt the witch-doctor had gone into the bush. He was a great witch-doctor. " Of course he's up to something," said Waterhouse, and became silent.

" But what can he do? " asked Pollock, unheeded.

" I must get you out of this. There's something brewing, or things would not be so quiet," said Waterhouse, after a gap of silence. Pollock wanted to know what the brew might be. " Dancing in a circle of skulls," said Waterhouse; " brewing a stink in a copper pot." Pollock wanted particulars. Waterhouse was vague, Pollock pressing. At last Waterhouse lost his temper. " How the devil should *I* know? " he said to Pollock's twentieth inquiry what the Porroh man would do. " He tried to kill you off-hand in the hut. *Now*, I fancy he will try something more elaborate. But you'll see fast enough. I don't want to help unnerve you. It's probably all nonsense."

That night, as they were sitting at their fire, Pollock again tried to draw Waterhouse out on the subject of Porroh methods. " Better get to sleep," said Waterhouse, when Pollock's bent became apparent; " we start early to-morrow. You may want all your nerve about you."

" But what line will he take? "

" Can't say. They're versatile people. They know a lot of rum dodges. You'd better get that copper-devil, Shakespear, to talk."

There was a flash and a heavy bang out of the darkness behind the huts, and a clay bullet came whistling close to Pollock's head. This, at least, was crude enough. The blacks and half-breeds sitting and yarning round their own fire jumped up, and some one fired into the dark.

" Better go into one of the huts," said Waterhouse quietly, still sitting unmoved.

Pollock stood up by the fire and drew his revolver.

Fighting, at least, he was not afraid of. But a man in the dark is in the best of armour. Realising the wisdom of Waterhouse's advice, Pollock went into the tent and lay down there.

What little sleep he had was disturbed by dreams, variegated dreams, but chiefly of the Porroh man's face, upside down, as he went out of the hut, and looked up under his arm. It was odd that this transitory impression should have stuck so firmly in Pollock's memory. Moreover, he was troubled by queer pains in his limbs.

In the white haze of the early morning, as they were loading the canoes, a barbed arrow suddenly appeared quivering in the ground close to Pollock's foot. The boys made a perfunctory effort to clear out the thicket, but it led to no capture.

After these two occurrences, there was a disposition on the part of the expedition to leave Pollock to himself, and Pollock became, for the first time in his life, anxious to mingle with blacks. Waterhouse took one canoe, and Pollock, in spite of a friendly desire to chat with Waterhouse, had to take the other. He was left all alone in the front part of the canoe, and he had the greatest trouble to make the men—who did not love him—keep to the middle of the river, a clear hundred yards or more from either shore. However, he made Shakespear, the Freetown half-breed, come up to his own end of the canoe and tell him about Porroh, which Shakespear, failing in his attempts to leave Pollock alone, presently did with considerable freedom and gusto.

The day passed. The canoe glided swiftly along the ribbon of lagoon water, between the drift of water-figs, fallen trees, papyrus, and palm-wine palms, and with the dark mangrove swamp to the left, through which one could hear now and then the roar of the Atlantic surf. Shakespear told in his soft, blurred English of how the Porroh could cast spells; how men withered up under their malice; how they could send dreams and devils; how they tormented and killed the sons of Ijibu; how they kidnapped a white trader from Sulyma who had maltreated one of the sect, and how his body looked when it was found. And Pollock after each narrative cursed under his breath at the want of missionary enterprise that allowed such things to be, and at the inert British Government that ruled over this dark heathendom of Sierra Leone. In the evening they came to the Kasi Lake, and sent a score of crocodiles lumbering off the island on which the expedition camped for the night.

The next day they reached Sulyma, and smelt the sea breeze, but Pollock had to put up there for five days before he could get on to Freetown. Waterhouse, considering him to be comparatively safe here, and within the pale of Freetown influence, left him and went back with the expedition to Gbemma, and Pollok became very friendly with Perera, the only resident white trader at Sulyma—so friendly, indeed, that he went about with him everywhere. Perera was a little Portuguese Jew, who had lived in England, and he appreciated the Englishman's friendliness as a great compliment.

For two days nothing happened out of the ordinary; for the most part Pollock and Perera played Nap— the only game they had in common—and Pollock got into debt. Then, on the second evening, Pollock had a disagreeable intimation of the arrival of the Porroh man in Sulyma by getting a flesh-wound in the shoulder from a lump of filed iron. It was a long shot, and the missile had nearly spent its force when it hit him. Still, it conveyed its message plainly enough. Pollock sat up in his hammock, revolver in hand, all that night, and next morning confided, to some extent, in the Anglo-Portuguese.

13

Perera took the matter seriously. He knew the local customs pretty thoroughly. " It is a personal question, you must know. It is revenge. And, of course, he is hurried by your leaving de country. None of de natives or half-breeds will interfere wid him very much— unless you make it wort deir while. If you come upon him suddenly, you might shoot him. But den he might shoot you.

" Den dere's dis—infernal magic," said Perera. " Of course I don't believe in it—superstition—but still it's not nice to tink dat wherever you are, dere is a black man, who spends a moonlight night now and den a-dancing about a fire to send you bad dreams. . . . Had any bad dreams? "

" Rather," said Pollock. " I keep on seeing the beggar's head upside down grinning at me and showing all his teeth as he did in the hut, and coming close up to me, and then going ever so far off, and coming back. It's nothing to be afraid of, but somehow it simply paralyses me with terror in my sleep. Queer things— dreams. I know it's a dream all the time, and I can't wake up from it."

" It's probably only fancy," said Perera. " Den my niggers say Porroh men can send snakes. Seen any snakes lately? "

" Only one. I killed him this morning, on the floor near my hammock. Almost trod on him as I got up."

" *Ah!* " said Perera, and then, reassuringly, " Of course it is a—coincidence. Still, I would keep my eyes open. Den dere's pains in de bones."

" I thought they were due to miasma," said Pollock.

" Probably dey are. When did dey begin? "

Then Pollock remembered that he first noticed them the night after the fight in the hut. " It's my opinion he don't want to kill you," said Perera—" at least not yet. I've heard deir idea is to scare and worry a man wid deir spells, and narrow misses, and rheumatic pains, and bad dreams, and all dat, until he's sick of life. Of course it's all talk, you know. You mustn't worry about it. . . . But I wonder what he'll be up to next."

" *I* shall have to be up to something first," said Pollock, staring gloomily at the greasy cards that Perera was putting on the table. " It don't suit my dignity to be followed about, and shot at, and blighted in this way. I wonder if Porroh hokey-pokey upsets your luck at cards."

He looked at Perera suspiciously.

" Very likely it does," said Perera warmly, shuffling. " Dey are wonderful people."

That afternoon Pollock killed two snakes in his hammock, and there was also an extraordinary increase in the number of red ants that swarmed over the place; and these annoyances put him in a fit temper to talk over business with a certain Mendi rough he had interviewed before. The Mendi rough showed Pollock a little iron dagger, and demonstrated where one struck in the neck, in a way that made Pollock shiver, and in return for certain considerations Pollock promised him a double-barrelled gun with an ornamental lock.

In the evening, as Pollock and Perera were playing cards, the Mendi rough came in through the doorway carrying something in a blood-soaked piece of native cloth.

" Not here! " said Pollock very hurriedly. " Not here! "

But he was not quick enough to prevent the man, who was anxious to get to Pollock's side of the bargain, from opening the cloth and throwing the head of the Porroh man upon the table. It bounded from there on to the floor, leaving a red trail on the cards, and rolled into a corner, where it came to rest upside down, but glaring hard at Pollock.

Perera jumped up as the thing fell among the cards, and began in his excitement to gabble in Portuguese.

The Mendi was bowing, with the red cloth in his hand. " De gun! " he said. Pollock stared back at the head in the corner. It bore exactly the expression it had in his dreams. Something seemed to snap in his own brain as he looked at it.

Then Perera found his English again.

" You got him killed? " he said. " You did not kill him yourself? "

" Why should I? " said Pollock.

" But he will not be able to take it off now! "

" Take *what* off? " said Pollock.

" And all dese cards are spoiled! "

" *What* do you mean by taking off? " said Pollock.

" You must send me a new pack from Freetown. You can buy dem dere."

" But—' take it off ? ' "

" It is only superstition. I forgot. De niggers say dat if de witches—he was a witch. . . . But it is rubbish. . . . You must make de Porroh man take it off, or kill him yourself. . . . It is very silly."

Pollock swore under his breath, still staring hard at the head in the corner.

" I can't stand that glare," he said. Then suddenly he rushed at the thing and kicked it. It rolled some yards or so, and came to rest in the same position as before, upside down, and looking at him.

" He is ugly," said the Anglo-Portuguese. " Very ugly. Dey do it on deir faces with little knives."

Pollock would have kicked the head again, but the Mendi man touched him on the arm. " De gun? " he said, looking nervously at the head.

" Two—if you will take that beastly thing away," said Pollock.

The Mendi shook his head, and intimated that he only wanted one gun now due to him, and for which he would be obliged. Pollock found neither cajolery nor bullying any good with him. Perera had a gun to sell (at a profit of three hundred per cent), and with that the man presently departed. Then Pollock's eyes, against his will, were recalled to the thing on the floor.

"It is funny dat his head keeps upside down," said Perera, with an uneasy laugh. "His brains must be heavy, like de weight in de little images one sees dat keep always upright wid lead in dem. You will take him wiv you when you go presently. You might take him now. De cards are all spoilt. Dere is a man sell dem in Freetown. De room is in a filthy mess as it is. You should have killed him yourself."

Pollock pulled himself together, and went and picked up the head. He would hang it up by the lamp-hook in the middle of the ceiling of his room, and dig a grave for it at once. He was under the impression that he hung it up by the hair, but that must have been wrong, for when he returned for it, it was hanging by the neck upside down.

He buried it before sunset on the north side of the shed he occupied, so that he should not have to pass the grave after dark when he was returning from Perera's. He killed two snakes before he went to sleep. In the darkest part of the night he awoke with a start, and heard a pattering sound and something scraping on the floor. He sat up noiselessly, and felt under his pillow for his revolver. A mumbling growl followed, and Pollock fired at the sound. There was a yelp, and something dark passed for a moment across the hazy blue of the doorway. "A dog!" said Pollock, lying down again.

In the early dawn he awoke again with a peculiar sense of unrest. The vague pain in his bones had returned. For some time he lay watching the red ants that were swarming over the ceiling, and then, as the light grew brighter, he looked over the edge of his hammock and saw something dark on the floor. He

17

gave such a violent start that the hammock overset and flung him out.

He found himself lying perhaps a yard away from the head of the Porroh man. It had been disinterred by the dog, and the nose was grievously battered. Ants and flies swarmed over it. By an odd coincidence it was still upside down, and with the same diabolical expression in the inverted eyes.

Pollock sat paralysed, and stared at the horror for some time. Then he got up and walked round it—giving it a wide berth—and out of the shed. The clear light of the sunrise, the living stir of vegetation before the breath of the dying land-breeze, and the empty grave with the marks of the dog's paws, lightened the weight upon his mind a little.

He told Perera of the business as though it was a jest—a jest to be told with white lips. "You should not have frighten de dog," said Perera, with poorly simulated hilarity.

The next two days, until the steamer came, were spent by Pollock in making a more effectual disposition of his possession. Overcoming his aversion to handling the thing he went down to the river mouth and threw it into the sea-water, but by some miracle it escaped the crocodiles, and was cast up by the tide on the mud a little way up the river, to be found by an intelligent Arab half-breed, and offered for sale to Pollock and Perera as a curiosity, just on the edge of night. The native hung about in the brief twilight, making lower and lower offers, and at last, getting scared in some way by the evident dread these wise white men had for the thing, went off, and passing Pollock's shed, threw his burden in there for Pollock to discover in the morning.

At this Pollock got into a kind of frenzy. He would burn the thing. He went out straightway into the dawn, and had constructed a big pyre of brushwood before the heat of the day. He was interrupted by the hooter of the little paddle steamer from Monrovia to Bathurst which was coming through the gap in the bar. "Thank Heaven!" said Pollock, with infinite piety, when the meaning of the sound dawned upon him. With trembling hands he lit his pile of wood hastily, threw the head upon it, and went away to pack his portmanteau and make his adieux to Perera.

That afternoon, with a sense of infinite relief, Pollock watched the flat swampy foreshore of the Sulyma grow small in the distance. The gap in the long line of white surge became narrower and narrower. It seemed to be closing in and cutting him off from his trouble. The feeling of dread and worry began to slip from him bit by bit. At Sulyma, belief in Porroh malignity and Porroh magic had been in the air, his sense of Porroh had been vast, pervading, threatening, dreadful. Now manifestly the domain of Porroh was only a little place, a little black band between the sea and the blue cloudy Mendi uplands.

"Good-bye, Porroh!" said Pollock. "Good-bye—certainly not *au revoir*."

The captain of the steamer came and leant over the rail beside him, and wished him good evening, and spat at the froth of the wake in token of friendly ease.

"I picked up a rummy curio on the beach this go," said the captain. "It's a thing I never saw done this side of Indy before."

"What might that be?" said Pollock.

"Pickled 'ed," said the captain.

"*What?*" said Pollock.

"'Ed—smoked. 'Ed of one of these Porroh chaps, all ornamented with knife-cuts. Why! What's up? Nothing? I shouldn't have took you for a nervous chap. Green in the face. By gosh! you're a bad sailor. All right, eh? Lord, how funny you went! . . .

Well, this 'ed I was telling you of is a bit rum in a way. I've got it, along with some snakes, in a jar of spirit in my cabin what I keeps for such curios, and I'm hanged if it don't float upsy down. Hallo! "

Pollock had given an incoherent cry, and had his hands in his hair. He ran towards the paddle-boxes with a half-formed idea of jumping into the sea, and then he realised his position and turned back towards the captain.

" Here! " said the captain. " Jack Philips, just keep him off me! Stand off! No nearer, mister! What's the matter with you? Are you mad? "

Pollock put his hand to his head. It was no good explaining. " I believe I am pretty nearly mad at times," he said. " It's a pain I have here. Comes suddenly. You'll excuse me, I hope."

He was white and in a perspiration. He saw suddenly very clearly all the danger he ran of having his sanity doubted. He forced himself to restore the captain's confidence by answering his sympathetic inquiries, noting his suggestions, even trying a spoonful of neat brandy in his cheek, and, that matter settled, asking a number of questions about the captain's private trade in curiosities. The captain described the head in detail. All the while Pollock was struggling to keep under a preposterous persuasion that the ship was as transparent as glass, and that he could distinctly see the inverted face looking at him from the cabin beneath his feet.

Pollock had a worse time almost on the steamer than he had at Sulyma. All day he had to control himself, in spite of his intense perception of the imminent presence of that horrible head that was overshadowing his mind. At night his old nightmare returned, until, with a violent effort, he would force himself awake, rigid with the horror of it, and with the ghost of a hoarse scream in his throat.

He left the actual head behind at Bathurst, where he changed ship for Teneriffe, but not his dreams nor the dull ache in his bones. At Teneriffe Pollock transferred to a Cape liner, but the head followed him. He gambled, he tried chess, he even read books, but he knew the danger of drink. Yet whenever a round black shadow, a round black object came into his range, there he looked for the head, and—saw it. He knew clearly enough that his imagination was growing traitor to him, and yet at times it seemed the ship he sailed in, his fellow-passengers, the sailors, the wide sea, was all part of a filmy phantasmagoria that hung, scarcely veiling it, between him and a horrible real world. Then the Porroh man, thrusting his diabolical face through that curtain, was the one real and undeniable thing. At that he would get up and touch things, taste something, gnaw something, burn his hand with a match, or run a needle into himself.

So, struggling grimly and silently with his excited imagination, Pollock reached England. He landed at Southampton, and went on straight from Waterloo to his banker's in Cornhill in a cab. There he transacted some business with the manager in a private room, and all the while the head hung like an ornament under the black marble mantel and dripped upon the fender. He could hear the drops fall, and see the red on the fender.

" A pretty fern," said the manager, following his eyes. " But it makes the fender rusty."

" Very," said Pollock; " a *very* pretty fern. And that reminds me. Can you recommend me a physician for mind troubles? I've got a little—what is it?— hallucination."

The head laughed savagely, wildly. Pollock was surprised the manager did not notice it. But the manager only stared at his face.

With the address of a doctor, Pollock presently

emerged in Cornhill. There was no cab in sight, and so he went on down to the western end of the street, and essayed the crossing opposite the Mansion House. The crossing is hardly easy even for the expert Londoner; cabs, vans, carriages, mail-carts, omnibuses go by in one incessant stream; to any one fresh from the malarious solitudes of Sierra Leone it is a boiling, maddening confusion. But when an inverted head suddenly comes bouncing, like an indiarubber ball, between your legs, leaving distinct smears of blood every time it touches the ground, you can scarcely hope to avoid an accident. Pollock lifted his feet convulsively to avoid it, and then kicked at the thing furiously. Then something hit him violently in the back, and a hot pain ran up his arm.

He had been hit by the pole of an omnibus, and three of the fingers of his left hand smashed by the hoof of one of the horses—the very fingers, as it happened, that he shot from the Porroh man. They pulled him out from between the horses' legs, and found the address of the physician in his crushed hand.

For a couple of days Pollock's sensations were full of the sweet, pungent smell of chloroform, of painful operations that caused him no pain, of lying still and being given food and drink. Then he had a slight fever, and was very thirsty, and his old nightmare came back. It was only when it returned that he noticed it had left him for a day.

" If my skull had been smashed instead of my fingers, it might have gone altogether," said Pollock, staring thoughtfully at the dark cushion that had taken on for the time the shape of the head.

Pollock at the first opportunity told the physician of his mind trouble. He knew clearly that he must go mad unless something should intervene to save him. He explained that he had witnessed a decapitation in Dahomey, and was haunted by one of the heads.

Naturally, he did not care to state the actual facts. The physician looked grave.

Presently he spoke hesitatingly. "As a child, did you get very much religious training?"

"Very little," said Pollock.

A shade passed over the physician's face. "I don't know if you have heard of the miraculous cures—it may be, of course, they are not miraculous—at Lourdes."

"Faith-healing will hardly suit me, I am afraid," said Pollock, with his eye on the dark cushion.

The head distorted its scarred features in an abominable grimace. The physician went upon a new track. "It's all imagination," he said, speaking with sudden briskness. "A fair case of faith-healing, anyhow. Your nervous system has run down, you're in that twilight state of health when the bogles come easiest. The strong impression was too much for you. I must make you up a little mixture that will strengthen your nervous system—especially your brain. And you must take exercise."

"I'm no good for faith-healing," said Pollock.

"And therefore we must restore tone. Go in search of stimulating air—Scotland, Norway, the Alps——"

"Jericho, if you like," said Pollock—"where Naaman went."

However, so soon as his fingers would let him, Pollock made a gallant attempt to follow out the doctor's suggestion. It was now November. He tried football, but to Pollock the game consisted in kicking a furious inverted head about a field. He was no good at the game. He kicked blindly, with a kind of horror, and when they put him back into goal, and the ball came swooping down upon him, he suddenly yelled and got out of its way. The discreditable stories that had driven him from England to wander in the tropics shut him off from any but men's society, and now his increasingly strange behaviour made even his man friends avoid him. The thing was no longer a thing of the eye merely; it gibbered at him, spoke to him. A horrible fear came upon him that presently, when he took hold of the apparition, it would no longer become some mere article of furniture, but would *feel* like a real dissevered head. Alone, he would curse at the thing, defy it, entreat it; once or twice, in spite of his firm self-control, he addressed it in the presence of others. He felt the growing suspicion in the eyes of the people that watched him—his landlady, the servant, his man.

One day early in December his cousin, Arnold—his next of kin—came to see him and draw him out, and watch his sunken yellow face with narrow, eager eyes. And it seemed to Pollock that the hat his cousin carried in his hand was no hat at all, but a Gorgon head that glared at him upside down, and fought with its eyes against his reason. However, he was still resolute to see the matter out. He got a bicycle, and, riding over the frosty road from Wandsworth to Kingston, found the thing rolling along at his side, and leaving a dark trail behind it. He set his teeth and rode faster. Then suddenly, as he came down the hill towards Richmond Park, the apparition rolled in front of him and under his wheel, so quickly that he had no time for thought, and turning quickly to avoid it, was flung violently against a heap of stones and broke his left wrist.

The end came on Christmas morning. All night he had been in a fever, the bandages encircling his wrist like a band of fire, his dreams more vivid and terrible than ever. In the cold, colourless, uncertain light that came before the sunrise, he sat up in his bed, and saw the head upon the bracket in the place of the bronze jar that had stood there overnight.

" I know that is a bronze jar," he said, with a chill doubt in his heart. Presently the doubt was irresistible. He got out of bed slowly, shivering, and advanced to the jar with his hand raised. Surely he would see now his imagination had deceived him, recognise the distinctive sheen of bronze. At last, after an age of hesitation, his fingers came down on the patterned cheek of the head. He withdrew them spasmodically. The last stage was reached. His sense of touch had betrayed him.

Trembling, stumbling against the bed, kicking against his shoes with his bare feet, a dark confusion eddying round him, he groped his way to the dressing-table, took his razor from the drawer, and sat down on the bed with this in his hand. In the looking-glass he saw his own face, colourless, haggard, full of the ultimate bitterness of despair.

He beheld in swift succession the incidents in the brief tale of his experience. His wretched home, his still more wretched schooldays, the years of vicious life he had led since then, one act of selfish dishonour leading to another; it was all clear and pitiless now, all its squalid folly, in the cold light of the dawn. He came to the hut, to the fight with the Porroh man, to the retreat down the river to Sulyma, to the Mendi assassin and his red parcel, to his frantic endeavours to destroy the head, to the growth of his hallucination. It was a hallucination! He *knew* it was. A hallucination merely. For a moment he snatched at hope. He looked away from the glass, and on the bracket the inverted head grinned and grimaced at him. . . . With the stiff fingers of his bandaged hand he felt at his neck for the throb of his arteries. The morning was very cold, the steel blade felt like ice.

IN THE AVU OBSERVATORY

THE observatory at Avu, in Borneo, stands on the spur of the mountain. To the north rises the old crater, black at night against the unfathomable blue of the sky. From the little circular building, with its mushroom dome, the slopes plunge steeply downward into the black mysteries of the tropical forest beneath. The little house in which the observer and his assistant live is about fifty yards from the observatory, and beyond this are the huts of their native attendants.

Thaddy, the chief observer, was down with a slight fever. His assistant, Woodhouse, paused for a moment in silent contemplation of the tropical night before commencing his solitary vigil. The night was very still. Now and then voices and laughter came from the native huts, or the cry of some strange animal was heard from the midst of the mystery of the forest. Nocturnal insects appeared in ghostly fashion out of the darkness and fluttered round his light. He thought, perhaps, of all the possibilities of discovery that still lay in the black tangle beneath him ; for to the naturalist the virgin forests of Borneo are still a wonderland full of strange questions and half-suspected discoveries. Woodhouse carried a small lantern in his hand, and its yellow glow contrasted vividly with the infinite series of tints between lavender-blue and black in which the landscape was painted. His hands and face were smeared with ointment against the attacks of the mosquitoes.

Even in these days of celestial photography, work done in a purely temporary erection, and with only the most primitive appliances in addition to the telescope, still involves a very large amount of cramped and motionless watching. He sighed as he thought of the physical fatigues before him, stretched himself, and entered the observatory.

The reader is probably familiar with the structure of an ordinary astronomical observatory. The building is usually cylindrical in shape, with a very light hemispherical roof capable of being turned round from the interior. The telescope is supported upon a stone pillar in the centre, and a clockwork arrangement compensates for the earth's rotation, and allows a star once found to be continuously observed. Besides this, there is a compact tracery of wheels and screws about its point of support, by which the astronomer adjusts it. There is, of course, a slit in the movable roof which follows the eye of the telescope in its survey of the heavens. The observer sits or lies on a sloping wooden arrangement, which he can wheel to any part of the observatory as the position of the telescope may require. Within it is advisable to have things as dark as possible, in order to enhance the brilliance of the stars observed.

The lantern flared as Woodhouse entered his circular den, and the general darkness fled into black shadows behind the big machine, from which it presently seemed to creep back over the whole place again as the light waned. The slit was a profound transparent blue, in which six stars shone with tropical brilliance, and their light lay, a pallid gleam, along the black tube of the instrument. Woodhouse shifted the roof, and then proceeding to the telescope, turned first one wheel and then another, the great cylinder slowly swinging into a new position. Then he glanced through the finder, the little companion telescope, moved the roof a little more, made some further adjustments, and set the clockwork in motion. He took off his jacket, for the night was very hot, and pushed into position the uncomfortable seat to which he was condemned for the next four hours. Then with a sigh he resigned himself to his watch upon the mysteries of space.

There was no sound now in the observatory, and the lantern waned steadily. Outside there was the occasional cry of some animal in alarm or pain, or calling to its mate, and the intermittent sounds of the Malay and Dyak servants. Presently one of the men began a queer chanting song, in which the others joined at intervals. After this it would seem that they turned in for the night, for no further sound came from their direction, and the whispering stillness became more and more profound.

The clockwork ticked steadily. The shrill hum of a mosquito explored the place and grew shriller in indignation at Woodhouse's ointment. Then the lantern went out and all the observatory was black.

Woodhouse shifted his position presently, when the slow movement of the telescope had carried it beyond the limits of his comfort.

He was watching a little group of stars in the Milky Way, in one of which his chief had seen or fancied a remarkable colour variability. It was not a part of the regular work for which the establishment existed, and for that reason perhaps Woodhouse was deeply interested. He must have forgotten things terrestrial. All his attention was concentrated upon the great blue circle of the telescope field—a circle powdered, so it seemed, with an innumerable multitude of stars, and all luminous against the blackness of its setting. As he watched he seemed to himself to become incorporeal, as if he too were floating in the ether of space. Infinitely remote was the faint red spot he was observing.

Suddenly the stars were blotted out. A flash of blackness passed, and they were visible again.

"Queer," said Woodhouse. "Must have been a bird."

The thing happened again, and immediately after

the great tube shivered as though it had been struck. Then the dome of the observatory resounded with a series of thundering blows. The stars seemed to sweep aside as the telescope—which had been unclamped—swung round and away from the slit in the roof.

"Great Scott!" cried Woodhouse. "What's this?"

Some huge vague black shape, with a flapping something like a wing, seemed to be struggling in the aperture of the roof. In another moment the slit was clear again, and the luminous haze of the Milky Way shone warm and bright.

The interior of the roof was perfectly black, and only a scraping sound marked the whereabouts of the unknown creature.

Woodhouse had scrambled from the seat to his feet. He was trembling violently and in a perspiration with the suddenness of the occurrence. Was the thing, whatever it was, inside or out? It was big, whatever else it might be. Something shot across the skylight, and the telescope swayed. He started violently and put his arm up. It was in the observatory, then, with him. It was clinging to the roof apparently. What the devil was it? Could it see him?

He stood for perhaps a minute in a state of stupefaction. The beast, whatever it was, clawed at the interior of the dome, and then something flapped almost into his face, and he saw the momentary gleam of starlight on a skin like oiled leather. His water-bottle was knocked off his little table with a smash.

The sense of some strange bird-creature hovering a few yards from his face in the darkness was indescribably unpleasant to Woodhouse. As his thought returned he concluded that it must be some night-bird or large bat. At any risk he would see what it was, and pulling a match from his pocket, he tried to strike it on the telescope seat. There was a smoking streak of phosphorescent light, the match flared for a moment, and he saw a vast wing sweeping towards him, a gleam of grey-brown fur, and then he was struck in the face and the match knocked out of his hand. The blow was aimed at his temple, and a claw tore sideways down to his cheek. He reeled and fell, and he heard the extinguished lantern smash. Another blow followed as he fell. He was partly stunned, he felt his own warm blood stream out upon his face. Instinctively he felt his eyes had been struck at, and, turning over on his face to save them, tried to crawl under the protection of the telescope.

He was struck again upon the back, and he heard his jacket rip, and then the thing hit the roof of the observatory. He edged as far as he could between the wooden seat and the eyepiece of the instrument, and turned his body round so that it was chiefly his feet that were exposed. With these he could at least kick. He was still in a mystified state. The strange beast banged about in the darkness, and presently clung to the telescope, making it sway and the gear rattle. Once it flapped near him, and he kicked out madly and felt a soft body with his feet. He was horribly scared now. It must be a big thing to swing the telescope like that. He saw for a moment the outline of a head black against the starlight, with sharply-pointed upstanding ears and a crest between them. It seemed to him to be as big as a mastiff's. Then he began to bawl out as loudly as he could for help.

At that the thing came down upon him again. As it did so his hand touched something beside him on the floor. He kicked out, and the next moment his ankle was gripped and held by a row of keen teeth. He yelled again, and tried to free his leg by kicking with the other. Then he realised he had the broken water-bottle at his hand, and snatching it, he struggled into a sitting posture, and feeling in the darkness towards his foot, gripped a velvety ear, like the ear of a big cat.

He had seized the water-bottle by its neck and brought it down with a shivering crash upon the head of the strange beast. He repeated the blow, and then stabbed and jabbed with the jagged end of it, in the darkness, where he judged the face might be.

The small teeth relaxed their hold, and at once Woodhouse pulled his leg free and kicked hard. He felt the sickening feel of fur and bone giving under his boot. There was a tearing bite at his arm, and he struck over it at the face, as he judged, and hit damp fur.

There was a pause; then he heard the sound of claws and the dragging of a heavy body away from him over the observatory floor. Then there was silence, broken only by his own sobbing breathing, and a sound like licking. Everything was black except the parallelogram of the blue skylight with the luminous dust of stars, against which the end of the telescope now appeared in silhouette. He waited, as it seemed, an interminable time.

Was the thing coming on again? He felt in his trouser-pocket for some matches, and found one remaining. He tried to strike this, but the floor was wet, and it spat and went out. He cursed. He could not see where the door was situated. In his struggle he had quite lost his bearings. The strange beast, disturbed by the splutter of the match, began to move again. "Time!" called Woodhouse, with a sudden gleam of mirth, but the thing was not coming at him again. He must have hurt it, he thought, with the broken bottle. He felt a dull pain in his ankle. Probably he was bleeding there. He wondered if it would support him if he tried to stand up. The night outside was very still. There was no sound of any one moving. The sleepy fools had not heard those wings battering upon the dome, nor his shouts. It was no good wasting strength in shouting. The monster flapped its wings and startled him into a defensive attitude. He hit his elbow against the seat, and it fell over with a crash. He cursed this, and then he cursed the darkness.

Suddenly the oblong patch of starlight seemed to sway to and fro. Was he going to faint? It would never do to faint. He clenched his fists and set his teeth to hold himself together. Where had the door got to? It occurred to him he could get his bearings by the stars visible through the skylight. The patch of stars he saw was in Sagittarius and south-eastward; the door was north—or was it north by west? He tried to think. If he could get the door open he might retreat. It might be the thing was wounded. The suspense was beastly. " Look here!" he said, " if you don't come on, I shall come at you."

Then the thing began clambering up the side of the observatory, and he saw its black outline gradually blot out the skylight. Was it in retreat? He forgot about the door and watched as the dome shifted and creaked. Somehow he did not feel very frightened or excited now. He felt a curious sinking sensation inside him. The sharply-defined patch of light, with the black form moving across it, seemed to be growing smaller and smaller. That was curious. He began to feel very thirsty, and yet he did not feel inclined to get anything to drink. He seemed to be sliding down a long funnel.

He felt a burning sensation in his throat, and then he perceived it was broad daylight, and that one of the Dyak servants was looking at him with a curious expression. Then there was the top of Thaddy's face upside down. Funny fellow, Thaddy, to go about like that! Then he grasped the situation better, and perceived that his head was on Thaddy's knee, and Thaddy was giving him brandy. And then he saw the eyepiece of the telescope with a lot of red smears on it. He began to remember.

" You've made this observatory in a pretty mess,"
said Thaddy.

The Dyak boy was beating up an egg in brandy.
Woodhouse took this and sat up. He felt a sharp
twinge of pain. His ankle was tied up, so were his arm
and the side of his face. The smashed glass, red-
stained, lay about the floor, the telescope seat was
overturned, and by the opposite wall was a dark pool.
The door was open, and he saw the grey summit of
the mountain against a brilliant background of blue
sky.

" Pah! " said Woodhouse. " Who's been killing
calves here? Take me out of it."

Then he remembered the Thing, and the fight he had
had with it.

" What *was* it? " he said to Thaddy—" the Thing
I fought with? "

" *You* know that best," said Thaddy. " But, anyhow,
don't worry yourself now about it. Have some more to
drink."

Thaddy, however, was curious enough, and it was a
hard struggle between duty and inclination to keep
Woodhouse quiet until he was decently put away in
bed, and had slept upon the copious dose of meat
extract Thaddy considered advisable. They then talked
it over together.

" It was," said Woodhouse, " more like a big bat
than anything else in the world. It had sharp, short
ears, and soft fur, and its wings were leathery. Its
teeth were little but devilish sharp, and its jaws could
not have been very strong or else it would have bitten
through my ankle."

" It has pretty nearly," said Thaddy.

" It seemed to me to hit out with its claws pretty
freely. That is about as much as I know about the
beast. Our conversation was intimate, so to speak,
and yet not confidential."

"The Dyak chaps talk about a Big Colugo, a Klang-utang—whatever that may be. It does not often attack man, but I suppose you made it nervous. They say there is a Big Colugo and a Little Colugo, and a something else that sounds like gobble. They all fly about at night. For my own part, I know there are flying foxes and flying lemurs about here, but they are none of them very big beasts."

"There are more things in heaven and earth," said Woodhouse—and Thaddy groaned at the quotation— "and more particularly in the forests of Borneo, than are dreamt of in our philosophies. On the whole, if the Borneo fauna is going to disgorge any more of its novelties upon me, I should prefer that it did so when I was not occupied in the observatory at night and alone."

THE FLOWERING OF THE STRANGE
ORCHID

THE buying of orchids always has in it a certain
speculative flavour. You have before you the brown
shrivelled limp of tissue, and for the rest you must trust
your judgment, or the auctioneer, or your good luck, as
your taste may incline. The plant may be moribund
or dead, or it may be just a respectable purchase, fair
value for your money, or perhaps—for the thing has
happened again and again—there slowly unfolds
before the delighted eyes of the happy purchaser, day
after day, some new variety, some novel richness, a
strange twist of labellum, or some subtler colouration
or unexpected mimicry. Pride, beauty, and profit
blossom together on one delicate green spike, and, it
may be, even immortality. For the new miracle
of nature may stand in need of a new specific name,
and what so convenient as that of its discoverer?
" Johnsmithia! " There have been worse names.

It was perhaps the hope of some such happy discovery
that made Winter-Wedderburn such a frequent atten-
dant at these sales—that hope, and also, maybe, the
fact that he had nothing else of the slightest interest
to do in the world. He was a shy, lonely, rather
ineffectual man, provided with just enough income to
keep off the spur of necessity, and not enough nervous
energy to make him seek any exacting employments.
He might have collected stamps or coins, or translated
Horace, or bound books, or invented new species of
diatoms. But as it happened, he grew orchids, and
had one ambitious little hothouse.

" I have a fancy," he said over his coffee, " that

something is going to happen to me to-day." He spoke
—as he moved and thought—slowly.

"Oh, don't say *that*!" said his housekeeper—who
was also his remote cousin. For "something happening" was a euphemism that meant only one thing to
her.

"You misunderstand me. I mean nothing unpleasant
. . . though what I do mean I scarcely know.

"To-day," he continued, after a pause, "Peters'
are going to sell a batch of plants from the Andamans
and the Indies. I shall go up and see what they have.
It may be I shall buy something good unawares. That
may be it."

He passed his cup for his second cupful of coffee.

"Are these the things collected by that poor young
fellow you told me of the other day?" asked his cousin,
as she filled his cup.

"Yes," he said, and became meditative over a piece
of toast.

"Nothing ever does happen to me," he remarked
presently, beginning to think aloud. "I wonder why?
Things enough happen to other people. There is
Harvey. Only the other week; on Monday he picked
up sixpence, on Wednesday his chicks all had the
staggers, on Friday his cousin came home from
Australia, and on Saturday he broke his ankle. What
a whirl of excitement!—compared to me."

"I think I would rather be without so much
excitement," said his housekeeper. "It can't be
good for you."

"I suppose it's troublesome. Still . . . you see,
nothing ever happens to me. When I was a little boy
I never had accidents. I never fell in love as I grew up.
Never married. . . . I wonder how it feels to have
something happen to you, something really remarkable.

"That orchid-collector was only thirty-six—twenty
years younger than myself—when he died. And he

had been married twice and divorced once; he had had malarial fever four times, and once he broke his thigh. He killed a Malay once, and once he was wounded by a poisoned dart. And in the end he was killed by jungle leeches. It must have all been very troublesome, but then it must have been very interesting, you know—except, perhaps, the leeches."

" I am sure it was not good for him," said the lady with conviction.

" Perhaps not." And then Wedderburn looked at his watch. " Twenty-three minutes past eight. I am going up by the quarter to twelve train, so that there is plenty of time. I think I shall wear my alpaca jacket —it is quite warm enough—and my grey felt hat and brown shoes. I suppose——"

He glanced out of the window at the serene sky and sunlit garden, and then nervously at his cousin's face.

" I think you had better take an umbrella if you are going to London," she said in a voice that admitted of no denial. " There's all between here and the station coming back."

When he returned he was in a state of mild excitement. He had made a purchase. It was rare that he could make up his mind quickly enough to buy, but this time he had done so.

" There are Vandas," he said, " and a Dendrobe and some Palæonophis." He surveyed his purchases lovingly as he consumed his soup. They were laid out on the spotless tablecloth before him, and he was telling his cousin all about them as he slowly meandered through his dinner. It was his custom to live all his visits to London over again in the evening for her and his own entertainment.

" I knew something would happen to-day. And I have bought all these. Some of them—some of them— I feel sure, do you know, that some of them will be remarkable. I don't know how it is, but I feel just as

37

sure as if some one had told me that some of these will turn out remarkable.

"That one"—he pointed to a shrivelled rhizome— "was not identified. It may be a Palæonophis—or it may not. It may be a new species, or even a new genus. And it was the last that poor Batten ever collected."

"I don't like the look of it," said his housekeeper. "It's such an ugly shape."

"To me it scarcely seems to have a shape."

"I don't like those things that stick out," said his housekeeper.

"It shall be put away in a pot to-morrow."

"It looks," said the housekeeper, "like a spider shamming dead."

Wedderburn smiled and surveyed the root with his head on one side. "It is certainly not a pretty lump of stuff. But you can never judge of these things from their dry appearance. It may turn out to be a very beautiful orchid indeed. How busy I shall be to-morrow! I must see to-night just exactly what to do with these things, and to-morrow, I shall set to work."

"They found poor Batten lying dead, or dying, in a mangrove swamp—I forget which," he began again presently, "with one of these very orchids crushed up under his body. He had been unwell for some days with some kind of native fever, and I suppose he fainted. These mangrove swamps are very unwholesome. Every drop of blood, they say, was taken out of him by the jungle-leeches. It may be that very plant that cost him his life to obtain."

"I think none the better of it for that."

"Men must work though women may weep," said Wedderburn with profound gravity.

"Fancy dying away from every comfort in a nasty swamp! Fancy being ill of fever with nothing to take but chlorodyne and quinine—if men were left to themselves they would live on chlorodyne and quinine

38

—and no one round you but horrible natives! They say the Andaman islanders are most disgusting wretches —and, anyhow, they can scarcely make good nurses, not having the necessary training. And just for people in England to have orchids!"

"I don't suppose it was comfortable, but some men seem to enjoy that kind of thing," said Wedderburn. "Anyhow, the natives of his party were sufficiently civilised to take care of all his collection until his colleague, who was an ornithologist, came back again from the interior; though they could not tell the species of the orchid, and had let it wither. And it makes these things more interesting."

"It makes them disgusting. I should be afraid of some of the malaria clinging to them. And just think, there has been a dead body lying across that ugly thing! I never thought of that before. There! I declare I cannot eat another mouthful of dinner."

"I will take them off the table if you like, and put them in the window-seat. I can see them just as well there."

The next few days he was indeed singularly busy in his steamy little hothouse, fussing about with charcoal, lumps of teak, moss, and all the other mysteries of the orchid cultivator. He considered he was having a wonderfully eventful time. In the evening he would talk about these new orchids to his friends, and over and over again he reverted to his expectation of something strange.

Several of the Vandas and the Dendrobium died under his care, but presently the strange orchid began to show signs of life. He was delighted, and took his housekeeper right away from jam-making to see it at once, directly he made the discovery.

"That is a bud," he said, "and presently there will be a lot of leaves there, and those little things coming out here are aerial rootlets."

"They look to me like little white fingers poking out of the brown," said his housekeeper. "I don't like them."

"Why not?"

"I don't know. They look like fingers trying to get at you. I can't help my likes and dislikes."

"I don't know for certain, but I don't *think* there are any orchids I know that have aerial rootlets quite like that. It may be my fancy, of course. You see they are a little flattened at the ends."

"I don't like 'em," said his housekeeper, suddenly shivering and turning away. "I know it's very silly of me—and I'm very sorry, particularly as you like the things so much. But I can't help thinking of that corpse."

"But it may not be that particular plant. That was merely a guess of mine."

His housekeeper shrugged her shoulders. "Anyhow, I don't like it," she said.

Wedderburn felt a little hurt at her dislike to the plant.

But that did not prevent his talking to her about orchids generally, and this orchid in particular, whenever he felt inclined.

"There are such queer things about orchids," he said one day; "such possibilities of surprises. You know, Darwin studied their fertilisation and showed that the whole structure of an ordinary orchid flower was contrived in order that moths might carry the pollen from plant to plant. Well, it seems that there are lots of orchids known, the flower of which cannot possibly be used for fertilisation in that way. Some of the Cypripediums, for instance; there are no insects known that can possibly fertilise them, and some of them have never been found with seed."

"But how do they form new plants?"

"By runners and tubers, and that kind of outgrowth.

That is easily explained. The puzzle is, what are the flowers for?

"Very likely," he added, "*my* orchid may be something extraordinary in that way. If so I shall study it. I have often thought of making researches as Darwin did. But hitherto I have not found the time, or something else has happened to prevent it. The leaves are beginning to unfold now. I do wish you would come and see them!"

But she said that the orchid-house was so hot it gave her the headache. She had seen the plant once again, and the aerial rootlets, which were now some of them more than a foot long, had unfortunately reminded her of tentacles reaching out after something; and they got into her dreams, growing after her with incredible rapidity. So that she had settled to her entire satisfaction that she would not see that plant again, and Wedderburn had to admire its leaves alone. They were of the ordinary broad form, and a deep glossy green, with splashes and dots of deep red towards the base. He knew of no other leaves quite like them. The plant was placed on a low bench near the thermometer, and close by was a simple arrangement by which a tap dripped on the hot-water pipes and kept the air steamy. And he spent his afternoons now with some regularity meditating on the approaching flowering of this strange plant.

And at last the great thing happened. Directly he entered the little glass house he knew that the spike had burst out, although his great *Palæonophis Lowii* hid the corner where his new darling stood. There was a new odour in the air, a rich, intensely sweet scent, that overpowered every other in that crowded, steaming little greenhouse.

Directly he noticed this he hurried down to the strange orchid. And, behold! the trailing green spikes bore now three great splashes of blossom, from which

41

this overpowering sweetness proceeded. He stopped before them in an ecstasy of admiration.

The flowers were white, with streaks of golden orange upon the petals; the heavy labellum was coiled into an intricate projection, and a wonderful bluish purple mingled there with the gold. He could see at once that the genus was altogether a new one. And the insufferable scent! How hot the place was! The blossoms swam before his eyes.

He would see if the temperature was right. He made a step towards the thermometer. Suddenly everything appeared unsteady. The bricks on the floor were dancing up and down. Then the white blossoms, the green leaves behind them, the whole greenhouse, seemed to sweep sideways, and then in a curve upward.

•　　　•　　　•　　　•　　　•

At half-past four his cousin made the tea, according to their invariable custom. But Wedderburn did not come in for his tea.

"He is worshipping that horrid orchid," she told herself, and waited ten minutes. "His watch must have stopped. I will go and call him."

She went straight to the hothouse, and, opening the door, called his name. There was no reply. She noticed that the air was very close, and loaded with an intense perfume. Then she saw something lying on the bricks between the hot-water pipes.

For a minute, perhaps, she stood motionless.

He was lying, face upward, at the foot of the strange orchid. The tentacle-like aerial rootlets no longer swayed freely in the air, but were crowded together, a tangle of grey ropes, and stretched tight, with their ends closely applied to his chin and neck and hands.

She did not understand. Then she saw from under one of the exultant tentacles upon his cheek there trickled a little thread of blood.

With an inarticulate cry she ran towards him, and tried to pull him away from the leech-like suckers. She snapped two of these tentacles, and their sap dripped red.

Then the overpowering scent of the blossom began to make her head reel. How they clung to him! She tore at the tough ropes, and he and the white inflorescence swam about her. She felt she was fainting, knew she must not. She left him and hastily opened the nearest door, and, after she had panted for a moment in the fresh air, she had a brilliant inspiration. She caught up a flower-pot and smashed in the windows at the end of the greenhouse. Then she re-entered. She tugged now with renewed strength at Wedderburn's motionless body, and brought the strange orchid crashing to the floor. It still clung with the grimmest tenacity to its victim. In a frenzy, she lugged it and him into the open air.

Then she thought of tearing through the sucker rootlets one by one, and in another minute she had released him and was dragging him away from the horror.

He was white and bleeding from a dozen circular patches.

The odd-job man was coming up the garden, amazed at the smashing of glass, and saw her emerge, hauling the inanimate body with red-stained hands. For a moment he thought impossible things.

"Bring some water!" she cried, and her voice dispelled his fancies. When, with unnatural alacrity, he returned with the water, he found her weeping with excitement, and with Wedderburn's head upon her knee, wiping blood from his face.

"What's the matter?" said Wedderburn, opening his eyes feebly, and closing them again at once.

"Go and tell Annie to come out here to me, and then go for Dr. Haddon at once," she said to the

43

odd-job man so soon as he brought the water; and added, seeing he hesitated, " I will tell you all about it when you come back."

Presently Wedderburn opened his eyes again, and, seeing that he was troubled by the puzzle of his position, she explained to him, " You fainted in the hothouse."

" And the orchid? "

" I will see to that," she said.

Wedderburn had lost a good deal of blood, but beyond that he had suffered no very great injury. They gave him brandy mixed with some pink extract of meat, and carried him upstairs to bed. His housekeeper told her incredible story in fragments to Dr. Haddon. " Come to the orchid-house and see," she said.

The cold outer air was blowing in through the open door, and the sickly perfume was almost dispelled. Most of the torn aerial rootlets lay already withered amidst a number of dark stains upon the bricks. The stem of the inflorescence was broken by the fall of the plant, and the flowers were growing limp and brown at the edges of the petals. The doctor stooped towards it, then saw that one of the aerial rootlets still stirred feebly, and hesitated.

The next morning the strange orchid still lay there, black now and putrescent. The door banged intermittently in the morning breeze, and all the array of Wedderburn's orchids was shrivelled and prostrate. But Weddeburn himself was bright and garrulous upstairs in the glory of his strange adventure.

THE RED ROOM

" I CAN assure you," said I, " that it will take a very tangible ghost to frighten me." And I stood up before the fire with my glass in my hand.

" It is your own choosing," said the man with the withered arm, and glanced at me askance.

" Eight-and-twenty years," said I, " I have lived, and never a ghost have I seen as yet."

The old woman sat staring hard into the fire, her pale eyes wide open. " Ay," she broke in; " and eight-and-twenty years you have lived and never seen the likes of this house, I reckon. There's a many things to see, when one's still but eight-and-twenty." She swayed her head slowly from side to side. " A many things to see and sorrow for."

I half suspected the old people were trying to enhance the spiritual terrors of their house by their droning insistence. I put down my empty glass on the table and looked about the room, and caught a glimpse of myself, abbreviated and broadened to an impossible sturdiness, in the queer old mirror at the end of the room. " Well," I said, " if I see anything to-night, I shall be so much the wiser. For I come to the business with an open mind."

" It's your own choosing," said the man with the withered arm once more.

I heard the sound of a stick and a shambling step on the flags in the passage outside, and the door creaked on its hinges as a second old man entered, more bent, more wrinkled, more aged even than the first. He supported himself by a single crutch, his eyes were covered by a shade, and his lower lip, half-averted, hung pale and pink from his decaying yellow teeth.

He made straight for an arm-chair on the opposite side of the table, sat down clumsily, and began to cough. The man with the withered arm gave this new-comer a short glance of positive dislike; the old woman took no notice of his arrival, but remained with her eyes fixed steadily on the fire.

" I said—it's your own choosing," said the man with the withered arm, when the coughing had ceased for a while.

" It's my own choosing," I answered.

The man with the shade became aware of my presence for the first time, and threw his head back for a moment and sideways, to see me. I caught a momentary glimpse of his eyes, small and bright and inflamed. Then he began to cough and splutter again.

" Why don't you drink? " said the man with the withered arm, pushing the beer towards him. The man with the shade poured out a glassful with a shaky arm that splashed half as much again on the deal table. A monstrous shadow of him crouched upon the wall and mocked his action as he poured and drank. I must confess I had scarce expected these grotesque custodians. There is to my mind something inhuman in senility, something crouching and atavistic; the human qualities seem to drop from old people insensibly day by day. The three of them made me feel uncomfortable, with their gaunt silences, their bent carriage, their evident unfriendliness to me and to one another.

" If," said I, " you will show me to this haunted room of yours, I will make myself comfortable there."

The old man with the cough jerked his head back so suddenly that it startled me, and shot another glance of his red eyes at me from under the shade; but no one answered me. I waited a minute, glancing from one to the other.

"If," I said a little louder, "if you will show me to this haunted room of yours, I will relieve you from the task of entertaining me."

"There's a candle on the slab outside the door," said the man with the withered arm, looking at my feet as he addressed me. "But if you go to the red room to-night——"

("This night of all nights!" said the old woman.)

"You go alone."

"Very well," I answered. "And which way do I go?"

"You go along the passage for a bit," said he, "until you come to a door, and through that is a spiral stair-case, and half-way up that is a landing and another door covered with baize. Go through that and down the long corridor to the end, and the red room is on your left up the steps."

"Have I got that right?" I said, and repeated his directions. He corrected me in one particular.

"And are you really going?" said the man with the shade, looking at me again for the third time, with that queer, unnatural tilting of the face.

("This night of all nights!" said the old woman.)

"It is what I came for," I said, and moved towards the door. As I did so, the old man with the shade rose and staggered round the table, so as to be closer to the others and to the fire. At the door I turned and looked at them, and saw they were all close together, dark against the firelight, staring at me over their shoulders, with an intent expression on their ancient faces.

"Good-night," I said, setting the door open.

"It's your own choosing," said the man with the withered arm.

I left the door wide open until the candle was well alight, and then I shut them in and walked down the chilly, echoing passage.

I must confess that the oddness of these three old

pensioners in whose charge her ladyship had left the castle, and the deep-toned, old-fashioned furniture of the housekeeper's room in which they foregathered, affected me in spite of my efforts to keep myself at a matter-of-fact phase. They seemed to belong to another age, an older age, an age when things spiritual were different from this of ours, less certain; an age when omens and witches were credible, and ghosts beyond denying. Their very existence was spectral; the cut of their clothing, fashions born in dead brains. The ornaments and conveniences of the room about them were ghostly—the thoughts of vanished men, which still haunted rather than participated in the world of to-day. But with an effort I sent such thoughts to the right-about. The long, draughty subterranean passage was chilly and dusty, and my candle flared and made the shadows cower and quiver. The echoes rang up and down the spiral staircase, and a shadow came sweeping up after me, and one fled before me into the darkness overhead. I came to the landing and stopped there for a moment, listening to a rustling that I fancied I heard; then, satisfied of the absolute silence, I pushed open the baize-covered door and stood in the corridor.

The effect was scarcely what I expected, for the moonlight coming in by the great window on the grand staircase picked out everything in vivid black shadow or silvery illumination. Everything was in its place; the house might have been deserted on the yesterday instead of eighteen months ago. There were candles in the sockets of the sconces, and whatever dust had gathered on the carpets or upon the polished flooring was distributed so evenly as to be invisible in the moonlight. I was about to advance, and stopped abruptly. A bronze group stood upon the landing, hidden from me by the corner of the wall, but its shadow fell with marvellous distinctness upon the white panelling and gave me the impression of some one crouching to waylay me. I stood rigid for half a minute perhaps. Then, with my hand in the pocket that held my revolver, I advanced, only to discover a Ganymede and Eagle glistening in the moonlight. That incident for a time restored my nerve, and a porcelain Chinaman on a buhl table, whose head rocked silently as I passed him, scarcely startled me.

The door to the red room and the steps up to it were in a shadowy corner. I moved my candle from side to side, in order to see clearly the nature of the recess in which I stood before opening the door. Here it was, thought I, that my predecessor was found, and the memory of that story gave me a sudden twinge of apprehension. I glanced over my shoulder at the Ganymede in the moonlight, and opened the door of the red room rather hastily, with my face half-turned to the pallid silence of the landing.

I entered, closed the door behind me at once, turned the key I found in the lock within, and stood with the candle held aloft, surveying the scene of my vigil, the great red room of Lorraine Castle, in which the young duke had died. Or, rather, in which he had begun his dying, for he had opened the door and fallen headlong down the steps I had just ascended. That had been the end of his vigil, of his gallant attempt to conquer the ghostly tradition of the place, and never, I thought, had apoplexy better served the ends of superstition. And there were other and older stories that clung to the room, back to the half-credible beginning of it all, the tale of a timid wife and the tragic end that came to her husband's jest of frightening her. And looking around that large sombre room, with its shadowy window bays, its recesses and alcoves, one could well understand the legends that had sprouted in its black corners, its germinating darkness. My candle was a little tongue of light in its vastness, that failed to pierce the opposite end of the room, and left an ocean of mystery and suggestion beyond its island of light.

I resolved to make a systematic examination of the place at once, and dispel the fanciful suggestions of its obscurity before they obtained a hold upon me. After satisfying myself of the fastening of the door, I began to walk about the room, peering round each article of furniture, tucking up the valances of the bed, and opening its curtains wide. I pulled up the blinds and examined the fastenings of the several windows before closing the shutters, leant forward and looked up the blackness of the wide chimney, and tapped the dark oak panelling for any secret opening. There were two big mirrors in the room, each with a pair of sconces bearing candles, and on the mantelshelf, too, were more candles in china candlesticks. All these I lit one after the other. The fire was laid, an unexpected consideration from the old housekeeper—and I lit it, to keep down any disposition to shiver, and when it was burning well, I stood round with my back to it and regarded the room again. I had pulled up a chintz-covered armchair and a table, to form a kind of barricade before me, and on this lay my revolver ready to hand. My precise examination had done me good, but I still found the remoter darkness of the place, and its perfect stillness, too stimulating for the imagination. The echoing of the stir and crackling of the fire was no sort of comfort to me. The shadow in the alcove at the end in particular had that undefinable quality of a presence, that odd suggestion of a lurking, living thing, that comes so easily in silence and solitude. At last, to reassure myself, I walked with a candle into it, and satisfied myself that there was nothing tangible there. I stood that candle upon the floor of the alcove, and left it in that position.

By this time I was in a state of considerable nervous tension, although to my reason there was no adequate cause for the condition. My mind, however, was perfectly clear. I postulated quite unreservedly that nothing supernatural could happen, and to pass the time I began to string some rhymes together, Ingoldsby fashion, of the original legend of the place. A few I spoke aloud, but the echoes were not pleasant. For the same reason I also abandoned, after a time, a conversation with myself upon the impossibility of ghosts and haunting. My mind reverted to the three old and distorted people downstairs, and I tried to keep it upon that topic. The sombre reds and blacks of the room troubled me; even with seven candles the place was merely dim. The one in the alcove flared in a draught, and the fire-flickering kept the shadows and penumbra perpetually shifting and stirring. Casting about for a remedy, I recalled the candles I had seen in the passage, and, with a slight effort, walked out into the moonlight, carrying a candle and leaving the door open, and presently returned with as many as ten. These I put in various knick-knacks of china with which the room was sparsely adorned, lit and placed where the shadows had lain deepest, some on the floor, some in the window recesses, until at last my seventeen candles were so arranged that not an inch of the room but had the direct light of at least one of them. It occurred to me that when the ghost came, I could warn him not to trip over them. The room was now quite brightly illuminated. There was something very cheery and reassuring in these little streaming flames, and snuffing them gave me an occupation, and afforded a helpful sense of the passage of time.

Even with that, however, the brooding expectation of the vigil weighed heavily upon me. It was after midnight that the candle in the alcove suddenly went out, and the black shadow sprang back to its place there. I did not see the candle go out; I simply turned and saw that the darkness was there, as one might start and see the unexpected presence of a stranger. " By Jove! " said I aloud; " that draught's a strong one! " and taking the matches from the table, I walked across the room in a leisurely manner to re-light the corner again. My first match would not strike, and as I succeeded with the second, something seemed to blink on the wall before me. I turned my head involuntarily, and saw that the two candles on the little table by the fireplace were extinguished. I rose at once to my feet.

" Odd! " I said. " Did I do that myself in a flash of absent-mindedness? "

I walked back, re-lit one, and as I did so, I saw the candle in the right sconce of one of the mirrors wink and go right out, and almost immediately its companion followed it. There was no mistake about it. The flame vanished, as if the wicks had been suddenly nipped between a finger and a thumb, leaving the wick neither glowing nor smoking, but black. While I stood gaping, the candle at the foot of the bed went out, and the shadows seemed to take another step towards me.

" This won't do! " said I, and first one and then another candle on the mantelshelf followed.

" What's up? " I cried, with a queer high note getting into my voice somehow. At that the candle on the wardrobe went out, and the one I had re-lit in the alcove followed.

" Steady on! " I said. " These candles are wanted," speaking with a half-hysterical facetiousness, and scratching away at a match the while for the mantel candlesticks. My hands trembled so much that twice I missed the rough paper of the matchbox. As the mantel emerged from darkness again, two candles in the remoter end of the window were eclipsed. But with the same match I also re-lit the larger mirror candles, and those on the floor near the doorway, so that for the moment I seemed to gain on the extinctions. But then in a volley there vanished four lights at once in different corners of the room, and I struck another match in quivering haste, and stood hesitating whither to take it.

As I stood undecided, an invisible hand seemed to sweep out the two candles on the table. With a cry of terror, I dashed at the alcove, then into the corner, and then into the window, re-lighting three, as two more vanished by the fireplace; then, perceiving a better way, I dropped the matches on the iron-bound deed-box in the corner, and caught up the bedroom candle-stick. With this I avoided the delay of striking matches; but for all that the steady process of extinction went on, and the shadows I feared and fought against returned, and crept in upon me, first a step gained on this side of me and then on that. It was like a ragged storm-cloud sweeping out the stars. Now and then one returned for a minute, and was lost again. I was now almost frantic with the horror of the coming darkness, and my self-possession deserted me. I leaped panting and dishevelled from candle to candle in a vain struggle against that remorseless advance.

I bruised myself on the thigh against the table, I sent a chair headlong, I stumbled and fell and whisked the cloth from the table in my fall. My candle rolled away from me, and I snatched another as I rose. Abruptly this was blown out, as I swung it off the table by the wind of my sudden movement, and immediately the two remaining candles followed. But there was light still in the room, a red light that staved off the shadows from me. The fire! Of course I could still thrust my candle between the bars and re-light it!

I turned to where the flames were still dancing between the glowing coals, and splashing red reflections upon the furniture, made two steps towards the grate, and incontinently the flames dwindled and vanished, the glow vanished, the reflections rushed together and vanished, and as I thrust the candle between the bars darkness close upon me like the shutting of an eye, wrapped about me in a stifling embrace, sealed my vision, and crushed the last vestiges of reason from my brain. The candle fell from my hand. I flung out my arms in a vain effort to thrust that ponderous blackness away from me, and, lifting up my voice, screamed with all my might—once, twice, thrice. Then I think I must have staggered to my feet. I know I thought suddenly of the moonlit corridor, and, with my head bowed and my arms over my face, made a run for the door.

But I had forgotten the exact position of the door, and struck myself heavily against the corner of the bed. I staggered back, turned, and was either struck or struck myself against some other bulky furniture. I have a vague memory of battering myself thus, to and fro in the darkness, of a cramped struggle, and of my own wild crying as I darted to and fro, of a heavy blow at last upon my forehead, a horrible sensation of falling that lasted an age, of my last frantic effort to keep my footing, and then I remember no more.

I opened my eyes in daylight. My head was roughly bandaged, and the man with the withered arm was watching my face. I looked about me, trying to remember what had happened, and for a space I could not recollect. I rolled my eyes into the corner, and saw the old woman, no longer abstracted, pouring out some drops of medicine from a little blue phial into a glass. "Where am I?" I asked; "I seem to remember you, and yet I cannot remember who you are."

They told me then, and I heard of the haunted Red Room as one who hears a tale. "We found you at dawn," said he, "and there was blood on your forehead and lips."

It was very slowly I recovered my memory of my

experience. "You believe now," said the old man, "that the room is haunted?" He spoke no longer as one who greets an intruder, but as one who grieves for a broken friend.

"Yes," said I; "the room is haunted."

"And you have seen it. And we, who have lived here all our lives, have never set eyes upon it. Because we have never dared. . . . Tell us, is it truly the old earl who——"

"No," said I; "it is not."

"I told you so," said the old lady, with the glass in her hand. "It is his poor young countess who was frightened——"

"It is not," I said. "There is neither ghost of earl nor ghost of countess in that room, there is no ghost there at all; but worse, far worse——"

"Well?" they said.

"The worst of all the things that haunt poor mortal man," said I; "and that is, in all its nakedness— *Fear!* Fear that will not have light nor sound, that will not bear with reason, that deafens and darkens and overwhelms. It followed me through the corridor, it fought against me in the room——"

I stopped abruptly. There was an interval of silence. My hand went up to my bandages.

Then the man with the shade sighed and spoke. "That is it," said he. "I knew that was it. A power of darkness. To put such a curse upon a woman! It lurks there always. You can feel it even in the day-time, even of a bright summer's day, in the hangings, in the curtains, keeping behind you however you face about. In the dusk it creeps along the corridor and follows you, so that you dare not turn. There is Fear in that room of hers—black Fear, and there will be— so long as this house of sin endures."

THE VALLEY OF SPIDERS

TOWARDS midday the three pursuers came abruptly round a bend in the torrent bed upon the sight of a very broad and spacious valley. The difficult and winding trench of pebbles along which they had tracked the fugitives for so long expanded to a broad slope, and with a common impulse the three men left the trail, and rode to a little eminence set with olive-dun trees, and there halted, the two others, as became them, a little behind the man with the silver-studded bridle.

For a space they scanned the great expanse below them with eager eyes. It spread remoter and remoter, with only a few clusters of sere thorn bushes here and there, and the dim suggestions of some now waterless ravine to break its desolation of yellow grass. Its purple distances melted at last into the bluish slopes of the further hills—hills it might be of a greener kind—and above them, invisibly supported, and seeming indeed to hang in the blue, were the snow-clad summits of mountains—that grew larger and bolder to the north-westward as the sides of the valley drew together. And westward the valley opened until a distant darkness under the sky told where the forests began. But the three men looked neither east nor west, but only steadfastly across the valley.

The gaunt man with the scarred lip was the first to speak. "Nowhere," he said, with a sigh of disappointment in his voice. "But after all, they had a full day's start."

"They don't know we are after them," said the little man on the white horse.

"*She* would know," said the leader bitterly, as if speaking to himself.

" Even then they can't go fast. They've got no beast but the mule, and all to-day the girl's foot has been bleeding——"

The man with the silver bridle flashed a quick intensity of rage on him. " Do you think I haven't seen that? " he snarled.

" It helps, anyhow," whispered the little man to himself.

The gaunt man with the scarred lip stared impassively. " They can't be over the valley," he said. " If we ride hard——"

He glanced at the white horse and paused.

" Curse all white horses! " said the man with the silver bridle, and turned to scan the beast his curse included.

The little man looked down between the melancholy ears of his steed.

" I did my best," he said.

The two others stared again across the valley for a space. The gaunt man passed the back of his hand across the scarred lip.

" Come up! " said the man who owned the silver bridle, suddenly. The little man started and jerked his rein, and the horse hoofs of the three made a multitudinous faint pattering upon the withered grass as they turned back towards the trail. . . .

They rode cautiously down the long slope before them, and so came through a waste of prickly twisted bushes and strange dry shapes of thorny branches that grew amongst the rocks, into the levels below. And there the trail grew faint, for the soil was scanty, and the only herbage was this scorched dead straw that lay upon the ground. Still, by hard scanning, by leaning beside the horses' necks and pausing ever and again, even these white men could contrive to follow after their prey.

There were trodden places, bent and broken blades

of the coarse grass, and ever and again the sufficient intimation of a footmark. And once the leader saw a brown smear of blood where the half-caste girl may have trod. And at that under his breath he cursed her for a fool.

The gaunt man checked his leader's tracking, and the little man on the white horse rode behind, a man lost in a dream. They rode one after another, the man with the silver bridle led the way, and they spoke never a word.

After a time it came to the little man on the white horse that the world was very still. He started out of his dream. Besides the little noises of their horses and equipment, the whole great valley kept the brooding quite of a painted scene.

Before him went his master and his fellow, each intently leaning forward to the left, each impassively moving with the paces of his horse; their shadows went before them—still, noiseless, tapering attendants; and nearer a crouched cool shape was his own. He looked about him. What was it had gone? Then he remembered the reverberation from the banks of the gorge and the perpetual accompaniment of shifting, jostling pebbles. And, moreover——? There was no breeze. That was it! What a vast, still place it was, a monotonous afternoon slumber! And the sky open and blank except for a sombre veil of haze that had gathered in the upper valley.

He straightened his back, fretted with his bridle, puckered his lips to whistle, and simply sighed. He turned in his saddle for a time, and stared at the throat of the mountain gorge out of which they had come. Blank! Blank slopes on either side, with never a sign of a decent beast or tree—much less a man. What a land it was! What a wilderness! He dropped again into his former pose.

It filled him with a momentary pleasure to see a wry

stick of purple black flash out into the form of a snake, and vanish amidst the brown. After all, the infernal valley *was* alive. And then, to rejoice him still more, came a little breath across his face, a whisper that came and went, the faintest inclination of a stiff black-antlered bush upon a little crest, the first intimations of a possible breeze. Idly he wetted his finger and held it up.

He pulled up sharply to avoid a collision with the gaunt man, who had stopped at fault upon the trail. Just at that guilty moment he caught his master's eye looking towards him.

For a time he forced an interest in the tracking. Then, as they rode on again, he studied his master's shadow and hat and shoulder, appearing and disappearing behind the gaunt man's nearer contours. They had ridden four days out of the very limits of the world into this desolate place, short of water, with nothing but a strip of dried meat under their saddles, over rocks and mountains, where surely none but these fugitives had ever been before—for *that*!

And all this was for a girl, a mere wilful child! And the man had whole cityfuls of people to do his basest bidding—girls, women! Why in the name of passionate folly *this* one in particular? asked the little man, and scowled at the world, and licked his parched lips with a blackened tongue. It was the way of the master, and that was all he knew. Just because she sought to evade him . . .

His eye caught a whole row of high-plumed canes bending in unison, and then the tails of silk that hung before his neck flapped and fell. The breeze was growing stronger. Somehow it took the stiff stillness out of things—and that was well.

" Hallo! " said the gaunt man.

All three stopped abruptly.

" What? " asked the master. " What? "

" Over there," said the gaunt man, pointing up the valley.

" What? "

" Something coming towards us."

And as he spoke a yellow animal crested a rise and came bearing down upon them. It was a big wild dog, coming before the wind, tongue out, at a steady pace, and running with such an intensity of purpose that he did not seem to see the horsemen he approached. He ran with his nose up, following, it was plain, neither scent nor quarry. As he drew nearer the little man felt for his sword. " He's mad," said the gaunt rider.

" Shout! " said the little man, and shouted.

The dog came on. Then when the little man's blade was already out, it swerved aside and went panting by them and passed. The eyes of the little man followed its flight. " There was no foam," he said. For a space the man with the silver-studded bridle stared up the valley. " Oh, come on! " he cried at last. " What does it matter? " and jerked his horse into movement again.

The little man left the insoluble mystery of a dog that fled from nothing but the wind, and lapsed into profound musings on human character. " Come on! " he whispered to himself. " Why should it be given to one man to say ' Come on!' with that stupendous violence of effect? Always, all his life, the man with the silver bridle has been saying that. If *I* said it——! " thought the little man. But people marvelled when the master was disobeyed even in the wildest things. This half-caste girl seemed to him, seemed to every one, mad—blasphemous almost. The little man, by way of comparison, reflected on the gaunt rider with the scarred lip, as stalwart as his master, as brave and, indeed, perhaps braver, and yet for him there was obedience, nothing but to give obedience duly and stoutly. . . .

Certain sensations of the hands and knees called the little man back to more immediate things. He became aware of something. He rode up beside his gaunt fellow. " Do you notice the horses? " he said in an undertone.

The gaunt face looked interrogation.

" They don't like this wind," said the little man, and dropped behind as the man with the silver bridle turned upon him.

" It's all right," said the gaunt-faced man.

They rode on again for a space in silence. The foremost two rode downcast upon the trail, the hindmost man watched the haze that crept down the vastness of the valley, nearer and nearer, and noted how the wind grew in strength moment by moment. Far away on the left he saw a line of dark bulks—wild hog, perhaps, galloping down the valley, but of that he said nothing, nor did he remark again upon the uneasiness of the horses.

And then he saw first one and then a second great white ball, a great shining white ball like a gigantic head of thistledown, that drove before the wind athwart the path. These balls soared high in the air, and dropped and rose again and caught for a moment, and hurried on and passed, but at the sight of them the restlessness of the horses increased.

Then presently he saw that more of these drifting globes—and then soon very many more—were hurrying towards him down the valley.

They became aware of a squealing. Athwart the path a huge boar rushed, turned his head but for one instant to glance at them, and then hurling on down the valley again. And at that all three stopped and sat in their saddles, staring into the thickening haze that was coming upon them.

" If it were not for this thistledown——" began the leader.

But now a big globe came drifting past within a score of yards of them. It was really not an even sphere at all, but a vast, soft, ragged, filmy thing, a sheet gathered by the corners, an aerial jelly-fish, as it were, but rolling over and over as it advanced, and trailing long cob-webby threads and streamers that floated in its wake.

" It isn't thistledown," said the little man.

" I don't like the stuff," said the gaunt man.

And they looked at one another.

" Curse it! " cried the leader. " The air's full of it up there. If it keeps on at this pace long, it will stop us altogether."

An instinctive feeling, such as lines out a herd of deer at the approach of some ambiguous thing, prompted them to turn their horses to the wind, ride forward a few paces, and stare at that advancing multitude of floating masses. They came on before the wind with a sort of smooth swiftness, rising and falling noiselessly, sinking to earth, rebounding high, soaring—all with a perfect unanimity, with a still, deliberate assurance.

Right and left of the horsemen the pioneers of this strange army passed. At one that rolled along the ground, breaking shapelessly and trailing out reluctantly into long grappling ribbons and bands, all three horses began to shy and dance. The master was seized with a sudden, unreasonable impatience. He cursed the drifting globes roundly. " Get on! " he cried; " get on! What do these things matter? How *can* they matter? Back to the trail! " He fell swearing at his horse and sawed the bit across its mouth.

He shouted aloud with rage. " I will follow that trail, I tell you," he cried. " Where is the trail? "

He gripped the bridle of his prancing horse and searched amidst the grass. A long and clinging thread fell across his face, a grey streamer dropped about his bridle arm, some big, active thing with many legs ran down the back of his head. He looked up to discover one of those grey masses anchored as it were above him by these things and flapping out ends as a sail flaps when a boat comes about—but noiselessly.

He had an impression of many eyes, of a dense crew of squat bodies, of long, many-jointed limbs hauling at their mooring ropes to bring the thing down upon him. For a space he stared up, reining in his prancing horse with the instinct born of years of horsemanship. Then the flat of a sword smote his back, and a blade flashed overhead and cut the drifting balloon of spider-web free, and the whole mass lifted softly and drove clear and away.

" Spiders! " cried the voice of the gaunt man. " The things are full of big spiders! Look, my lord! "

The man with the silver bridle still followed the mass that drove away.

" Look, my lord! "

The master found himself staring down at a red smashed thing on the ground that, in spite of partial obliteration, could still wriggle unavailing legs. Then, when the gaunt man pointed to another mass that bore down upon them, he drew his sword hastily. Up the valley now it was like a fog bank torn to rags. He tried to grasp the situation.

" Ride for it! " the little man was shouting. " Ride for it down the valley."

What happened then was like the confusion of a battle. The man with the silver bridle saw the little man go past him, slashing furiously at imaginary cobwebs, saw him cannon into the horse of the gaunt man and hurl it and its rider to earth. His own horse went a dozen paces before he could rein it in. Then he looked up to avoid imaginary dangers, and then back again to see a horse rolling on the ground, the gaunt man standing and slashing over it at a rent and fluttering mass of grey that streamed and wrapped about them both. And thick and fast as thistledown on waste land on a windy day in July the cobweb masses were coming on.

The little man had dismounted, but he dared not release his horse. He was endeavouring to lug the struggling brute back with the strength of one arm, while with the other he slashed aimlessly. The tentacles of a second grey mass had entangled themselves with the struggle, and this second grey mass came to its moorings, and slowly sank.

The master set his teeth, gripped his bridle, lowered his head, and spurred his horse forward. The horse on the ground rolled over, there was blood and moving shapes upon the flanks, and the gaunt man suddenly leaving it, ran forward towards his master, perhaps ten paces. His legs were swathed and encumbered with grey; he made ineffectual movements with his sword. Grey streamers waved from him; there was a thin grey veil across his face. With his left hand he beat at something on his body, and suddenly he stumbled and fell. He struggled to rise, and fell again and suddenly, horribly, began to howl, " Oh—ohoo, ohooh! "

The master could see the great spiders upon him, and others upon the ground.

As he strove to force his horse nearer to this gesticulating, screaming grey object that struggled up and down, there came a clatter of hoofs, and the little man, in the act of mounting, swordless, balanced on his belly athwart the white horse, and clutching its mane, whirled past. And again a clinging thread of grey gossamer swept across the master's face. All about him, and over him, it seemed this drifting, noiseless cobweb circled and drew near him. . . .

To the day of his death he never knew just how the event of that moment happened. Did he, indeed, turn his horse, or did it really of its own accord stampede after its fellow? Suffice it that in another second he was galloping full tilt down the valley with his sword whirling furiously overhead. And all about him on the quickening breeze, the spiders' air-ships, their air bundles and air sheets, seemed to him to hurry in a conscious pursuit.

Clatter, clatter, thud, thud—the man with the silver bridle rode, heedless of his direction, with his fearful face looking up now right, now left, and his sword arm ready to slash. And a few hundred yards ahead of him, with a trail of torn cobweb trailing behind him, rode the little man on the white horse, still but imperfectly in the saddle. The reeds bent before them, the wind blew fresh and strong, over his shoulder the master could see the webs hurrying to overtake. . . .

He was so intent to escape the spiders' webs that only as his horse gathered together for a leap did he realise the ravine ahead. And then he realised it only to misunderstand and interfere. He was leaning forward on his horse's neck and sat up and back all too late.

But if in his excitement he had failed to leap, at any rate he had not forgotten how to fall. He was horseman again in mid-air. He came off clear with a mere bruise upon his shoulder, and his horse rolled, kicking spasmodic legs, and lay still. But the master's sword drove its point into the hard soil, and snapped clean across, as though Chance refused him any longer as her Knight, and the splintered end missed his face by an inch or so.

He was on his feet in a moment, breathlessly scanning the on-rushing spider-webs. For a moment he was minded to run, and then thought of the ravine, and turned back. He ran aside once to dodge one drifting terror, and then he was swiftly clambering down the precipitous sides, and out of the touch of the gale.

There, under the lee of the dry torrent's steeper banks, he might crouch and watch these strange, grey masses pass and pass in safety till the wind fell, and it became possible to escape. And there for a long time he crouched, watching the strange, grey, ragged masses trail their streamers across his narrowed sky.

Once a stray spider fell into the ravine close beside him—a full foot it measured from leg to leg and its body was half a man's hand—and after he had watched its monstrous alacrity of search and escape for a little while and tempted it to bite his broken sword, he lifted up his iron-heeled boot and smashed it into a pulp. He swore as he did so, and for a time sought up and down for another.

Then presently, when he was surer these spider swarms could not drop into the ravine, he found a place where he could sit down, and sat and fell into deep thought and began, after his manner, to gnaw his knuckles and bite his nails. And from this he was moved by the coming of the man with the white horse.

He heard him long before he saw him, as a clattering of hoofs, stumbling footsteps, and a reassuring voice. Then the little man appeared, a rueful figure, still with a tail of white cobweb trailing behind him. They approached each other without speaking, without a salutation. The little was man fatigued and shamed to the pitch of hopeless bitterness, and came to a stop at last, face to face with his seated master. The latter winced a little under his dependent's eye. " Well? " he said at last, with no pretence of authority.

" You left him? "

" My horse bolted."

" I know. So did mine."

He laughed at his master mirthlessly.

" I say my horse bolted," said the man who once had a silver-studded bridle.

" Cowards both," said the little man.

The other gnawed his knuckle through some meditative moments, with his eye on his inferior.

"Don't call me a coward," he said at length.

"You are a coward, like myself."

"A coward possibly. There is a limit beyond which every man must fear. That I have learnt at last. But not like yourself. That is where the difference comes in."

"I never could have dreamt you would have left him. He saved your life two minutes before. . . . Why are you our lord?"

The master gnawed his knuckles again, and his countenance was dark.

"No man calls me a coward," he said. "No. . . . A broken sword is better than none. . . . One spavined white horse cannot be expected to carry two men a four days' journey. I hate white horses, but this time it cannot be helped. You begin to understand me? I perceive that you are minded, on the strength of what you have seen and fancy, to taint my reputation. It is men of your sort who unmake kings. Besides which—I never liked you."

"My lord!" said the little man.

"No," said the master. "*No!*"

He stood up sharply as the little man moved. For a minute perhaps they faced one another. Overhead the spiders' balls went driving. There was a quick movement among the pebbles; a running of feet, a cry of despair, a gasp and a blow. . . .

Towards nightfall the wind fell. The sun set in a calm serenity, and the man who had once possessed the silver bridle came at last very cautiously and by an easy slope out of the ravine again; but now he led the white horse that once belonged to the little man. He would have gone back to his horse to get his silver-mounted bridle again, but he feared night and a quickening breeze might still find him in the valley, and besides, he disliked greatly to think he might discover his horse all swathed in cobwebs and perhaps unpleasantly eaten.

And as he thought of those cobwebs, and of all the dangers he had been through, and the manner in which he had been preserved that day, his hand sought a little reliquary that hung about his neck, and he clasped it for a moment with heartfelt gratitude. As he did so his eyes went across the valley.

" I was hot with passion," he said, " and now she has met her reward. They also, no doubt——"

And behold! far away out of the wooded slopes across the valley, but in the clearness of the sunset, distinct and unmistakable, he saw a little spire of smoke.

At that his expression of serene resignation changed to an amazed anger. Smoke? He turned the head of the white horse about, and hesitated. And as he did so a little rustle of air went through the grass about him. Far away upon some reeds swayed a tattered sheet of grey. He looked at the cobwebs; he looked at the smoke.

" Perhaps, after all, it is not them," he said at last. But he knew better.

After he had stared at the smoke for some time, he mounted the white horse.

As he rode, he picked his way amidst stranded masses of web. For some reason there were many dead spiders on the ground, and those that lived feasted guiltily on their fellows. At the sound of his horse's hoofs they fled.

Their time had passed. From the ground, without either a wind to carry them or a winding-sheet ready, these things, for all their poison, could do him little evil.

He flicked with his belt at those he fancied came too near. Once, where a number ran together over a bare place, he was minded to dismount and trample them with his boots, but this impulse he overcame. Ever and again he turned in his saddle, and looked back at the smoke.

"Spiders," he muttered over and over again. "Spiders. Well, well . . . The next time I must spin a web."

THE EMPIRE OF THE ANTS

I

When Captain Gerilleau received instructions to take his new gunboat, the *Benjamin Constant*, to Badama on the Batemo arm of the Guaramadema and there assist the inhabitants against a plague of ants, he suspected the authorities of mockery. His promotion had been romantic and irregular, the affections of a prominent Brazilian lady and the captain's liquid eyes had played a part in the process, and the *Diario* and *O Futuro* had been lamentably disrespectful in their comments. He felt he was to give further occasion for disrespect.

He was a Creole, his conceptions of etiquette and discipline were pure-blooded Portuguese, and it was only to Holroyd, the Lancashire engineer who had come over with the boat, and as an exercise in the use of English—his " th" sounds were very uncertain— that he opened his heart.

" It is in effect," he said, " to make me absurd! What can a man do against ants? Dey come, dey go."

" They say," said Holroyd, " that these don't go. That chap you said was a Sambo——"

" Zambo;—it is a sort of mixture of blood."

" Sambo. He said the people are going! "

The captain smoked fretfully for a time. " Dese tings 'ave to happen," he said at last. " What is it? Plagues of ants and suchlike as God wills. Dere was a plague in Trinidad—the little ants that carry leaves.

All der orange-trees, all der mangoes! What does it matter? Sometimes ant armies come into your houses —fighting ants; a different sort. You go and they clean the house. Then you come back again;—the house is clean, like new! No cockroaches, no fleas, no jiggers in the floor."

"That Sambo chap," said Holroyd, "says these are a different sort of ant."

The captain shrugged his shoulders, fumed, and gave his attention to a cigarette.

Afterwards he reopened the subject. "My dear 'Olroyd, what am I to do about dese infernal ants?"

The captain reflected. "It is ridiculous," he said. But in the afternoon he put on his full uniform and went ashore, and jars and boxes came back to the ship and subsequently he did. And Holroyd sat on deck in the evening coolness and smoked profoundly and marvelled at Brazil. They were six days up the Amazon, some hundreds of miles from the ocean, and east and west of him there was a horizon like the sea, and to the south nothing but a sand-bank island with some tufts of scrub. The water was always running like a sluice, thick with dirt, animated with crocodiles and hovering birds, and fed by some inexhaustible source of tree trunks; and the waste of it, the headlong waste of it, filled his soul. The town of Alemquer, with its meagre church, its thatched sheds for houses, its discoloured ruins of ampler days, seemed a little thing lost in this wilderness of Nature, a sixpence dropped on Sahara. He was a young man, this was his first sight of the tropics, he came straight from England, where Nature is hedged, ditched, and drained into the perfection of submission, and he had suddenly discovered the insignificance of man. For six days they had been steaming up from the sea by unfrequented channels, and man had been as rare as a rare butterfly. One saw one day a canoe, another day a distant station, the next no men at all. He began to perceive that man is indeed a rare animal, having but a precarious hold upon this land.

He perceived it more clearly as the days passed, and he made his devious way to the Batemo, in the company of this remarkable commander, who ruled over one big gun, and was forbidden to waste his ammunition. Holroyd was learning Spanish industriously, but he was still in the present tense and substantive stage of speech, and the only other person who had any words of English was a negro stoker, who had them all wrong. The second in command was a Portuguese, da Cunha, who spoke French, but it was a different sort of French from the French Holroyd had learnt in Southport, and their intercourse was confined to politenesses and simple propositions about the weather. And the weather, like everything else in this amazing new world, the weather had no human aspect, and was hot by night and hot by day, and the air steam, even the wind was hot steam, smelling of vegetation in decay: and the alligators and the strange birds, the flies of many sorts and sizes, the beetles, the ants, the snakes, and monkeys seemed to wonder what man was doing in an atmosphere that had no gladness in its sunshine and no coolness in its night. To wear clothing was intolerable, but to cast it aside was to scorch by day, and expose an ampler area to the mosquitoes by night; to go on deck by day was to be blinded by glare and to stay below was to suffocate. And in the daytime came certain flies, extremely clever and noxious about one's wrist and ankle. Captain Gerilleau, who was Holroyd's sole distraction from these physical distresses, developed into a formidable bore, telling the simple story of his heart's affections day by day, a string of anonymous women, as if he were telling beads. Sometimes he suggested sport, and they shot at alligators, and at rare intervals they came to human aggregations in the waste of trees, and stayed for a day or so, and drank and sat about, and, one night, danced with Creole girls, who found Holroyd's poor elements of Spanish, without either past tense or future, amply sufficient for their purposes. But these were mere luminous chinks in the long grey passage of the streaming river, up which the throbbing engines beat. A certain liberal heathen deity, in the shape of a demi-john, held seductive court aft, and, it is probable, forward.

But Gerilleau learnt things about the ants, more things and more, at this stopping-place and that, and became interested in his mission.

" Dey are a new sort of ant," he said. " We have got to be—what do you call it?—entomologie? Big. Five centimetres! Some bigger! It is ridiculous. We are like the monkeys—sent to pick insects. . . . But dey are eating up the country."

He burst out indignantly. " Suppose—suddenly, there are complications with Europe. Here am I— soon we shall be above the Rio Negro—and my gun, useless ! "

He nursed his knee and mused.

" Dose people who were dere at de dancing place, dey 'ave come down. Dey 'ave lost all they got. De ants come to deir house one afternoon. Every one run out. You know when de ants come one must—every one runs out and they go over the house. If you stayed they'd eat you. See? Well, presently dey go back; dey say, ' The ants 'ave gone.' . . . De ants *aven't* gone. Dey try to go in—de son, 'e goes in. De ants fight."

" Swarm over him? "

" Bite 'im. Presently he comes out again—screaming and running. He runs past them to the river. See? He gets into de water and drowns de ants—yes." Gerilleau paused, brought his liquid eyes close to

Holroyd's face, tapped Holroyd's knee with his knuckle. "That night he dies, just as if he was stung by a snake."

"Poisoned by the ants?"

"Who knows?" Gerilleau shrugged his shoulders. "Perhaps they bit him badly. . . . When I joined dis service I joined to fight men. Dese things, dese ants, dey come and go. It is no business for men."

After that he talked frequently of the ants to Holroyd, and whenever they chanced to drift against any speck of humanity in that waste of water and sunshine and distant trees, Holroyd's improving knowledge of the language enabled him to recognise the ascendant word *Saüba*, more and more completely dominating the whole.

He perceived the ants were becoming interesting, and the nearer he drew to them the more interesting they became. Gerilleau abandoned his old themes almost suddenly, and the Portuguese lieutenant became a conversational figure; he knew something about the leaf-cutting ant, and expanded his knowledge. Gerilleau sometimes rendered what he had to tell to Holroyd. He told of the little workers that swarm and fight, and the big workers that command and rule, and how these latter always crawled to the neck and how their bites drew blood. He told how they cut leaves and made fungus beds, and how their nests in Caracas are sometimes a hundred yards across. Two days the three men spent disputing whether ants have eyes. The discussion grew dangerously heated on the second afternoon, and Holroyd saved the situation by going ashore in a boat to catch ants and see. He captured various specimens and returned, and some had eyes and some hadn't. Also, they argued, do ants bite or sting?

"Dese ants," said Gerilleau, after collecting information at a rancho, "have big eyes. They don't run

74

about blind—not as most ants do. No! Dey get in corners and watch what you do."

" And they sting? " asked Holroyd.

" Yes. Dey sting. Dere is poison in the sting." He meditated. " I do not see what men can do against ants. Dey come and go."

" But these don't go."

" They will," said Gerilleau.

Past Tamandu there is a long low coast of eighty miles without any population, and then one comes to the confluence of the main river and the Batemo arm like a great lake, and then the forest came nearer, came at last intimately near. The character of the channel changes, snags abound, and the *Benjamin Constant* moored by a cable that night, under the very shadow of dark trees. For the first time for many days came a spell of coolness, and Holroyd and Gerilleau sat late, smoking cigars and enjoying this delicious sensation. Gerilleau's mind was full of ants and what they could do. He decided to sleep at last, and lay down on a mattress on deck, a man hopelessly perplexed, his last words, when he already seemed asleep, were to ask, with a flourish of despair, " What can one do with ants? . . . De whole thing is absurd."

Holroyd was left to scratch his bitten wrists, and meditate alone.

He sat on the bulwark and listened to the little changes in Gerilleau's breathing until he was fast asleep, and then the ripple and lap of the stream took his mind, and brought back that sense of immensity that had been growing upon him since first he had left Para and come up the river. The monitor showed but one small light, and there was first a little talking forward and then stillness. His eyes went from the dim black outlines of the middle works of the gunboat towards the bank, to the black overwhelming mysteries of forest, lit now and then by a fire-fly, and never still from the murmur of alien and mysterious activities. . . .

It was the inhuman immensity of this land that astonished and oppressed him. He knew the skies were empty of men, the stars were specks in an incredible vastness of space; he knew the ocean was enormous and untamable, but in England he had come to think of the land as man's. In England it is indeed man's, the wild things live by sufferance, grow on lease, everywhere the roads, the fences, and absolute security runs. In an atlas, too, the land is man's, and all coloured to show his claim to it—in vivid contrast to the universal independent blueness of the sea. He had taken it for granted that a day would come when everywhere about the earth, plough and culture, light tramways and good roads, and ordered security, would prevail. But now, he doubted.

This forest was interminable, it had an air of being invincible, and Man seemed at best an infrequent precarious intruder. One travelled for miles, amidst the still, silent struggle of giant trees, of strangulating creepers, of assertive flowers, everywhere the alligator, the turtle, and endless varieties of birds and insects seemed at home, dwelt irreplaceably—but man, man at most held a footing upon resentful clearings, fought weeds, fought beasts and insects for the barest foothold, fell a prey to snake and beast, insect and fever, and was presently carried away. In many places down the river he had been manifestly driven back, this deserted creek or that preserved the name of a *casa*, and here and there ruinous white walls and a shattered tower enforced the lesson. The puma, the jaguar, were more the masters here. . . .

Who were the real masters?

In a few miles of this forest there must be more ants than there are men in the whole world! This seemed to Holroyd a perfectly new idea. In a few thousand years men had emerged from barbarism to a stage of civilisation that made them feel lords of the future and masters of the earth! But what was to prevent the ants evolving also? Such ants as one knew lived in little communities of a few thousand individuals, made no concerted efforts against the greater world. But they had a language, they had an intelligence! Why should things stop at that any more than men had stopped at the barbaric stage? Suppose presently the ants began to store knowledge, just as men had done by means of books and records, use weapons, form great empires, sustain a planned and organised war?

Things came back to him that Gerilleau had gathered about these ants they were approaching. They used a poison like the poison of snakes. They obeyed greater leaders even as the leaf-cutting ants do. They were carnivorous, and where they came they stayed. . . .

The forest was very still. The water lapped incessantly against the side. About the lantern overhead there eddied a noiseless whirl of phantom moths.

Gerilleau stirred in the darkness and sighed. " What can one *do*? " he murmured, and turned over and was still again.

Holroyd was roused from meditations that were becoming sinister by the hum of a mosquito.

2

The next morning Holroyd learned they were within forty kilometres of Badama, and his interest in the banks intensified. He came up whenever an opportunity offered to examine his surroundings. He could see no signs of human occupation whatever, save for a weedy ruin of a house and the green-stained façade of the long-deserted monastery at Moju, with a forest tree growing out of a vacant window space, and great creepers netted across its vacant portals. Several flights of strange yellow butterflies with semi-transparent wings crossed the river that morning, and many alighted on the monitor and were killed by the men. It was towards afternoon that they came upon the derelict *cuberta*.

She did not at first appear to be derelict; both her sails were set and hanging slack in the afternoon calm, and there was the figure of a man sitting on the fore planking beside the shipped sweeps. Another man appeared to be sleeping face downwards on the sort of longitudinal bridge these big canoes have in the waist. But it was presently apparent, from the sway of her rudder and the way she drifted into the course of the gunboat, that something was out of order with her. Gerilleau surveyed her through a field-glass, and became interested in the queer darkness of the face of the sitting man, a red-faced man he seemed, without a nose—crouching he was rather than sitting, and the longer the captain looked the less he liked to look at him, and the less able he was to take his glasses away.

But he did so at last, and went a little way to call up Holroyd. Then he went back to hail the cuberta. He hailed her again, and so she drove past him. *Santa Rosa* stood out clearly as her name.

As she came by and into the wake of the monitor, she pitched a little, and suddenly the figure of the crouching man collapsed as though all its joints had given way. His hat fell off, his head was not nice to look at, and his body flopped lax and rolled out of sight behind the bulwarks.

" Caramba! " cried Gerilleau, and resorted to Holroyd forthwith.

Holroyd was half-way up the companion. " Did you see dat? " said the captain.

" Dead! " said Holroyd. " Yes. You'd better send a boat aboard. There's something wrong."

" Did you—by any chance see—his face? "

"What was it like?"

"It was—ugh!—I have no words." And the captain suddenly turned his back on Holroyd and became an active and strident commander.

The gunboat came about, steamed parallel to the erratic course of the canoe, and dropped the boat with Lieutenant da Cunha and three sailors to board her. Then the curiosity of the captain made him draw up almost alongside as the lieutenant got aboard, so that the whole of the *Santa Rosa*, deck and hold, was visible to Holroyd.

He saw now clearly that the sole crew of the vessel was these two dead men, and though he could not see their faces, he saw by their outstretched hands, which were all of ragged flesh, that they had been subjected to some strange exceptional process of decay. For a moment his attention concentrated on those two enigmatical bundles of dirty clothes and laxly flung limbs, and then his eyes went forward to discover the open hold piled high with trunks and cases, and aft, to where the little cabin gaped inexplicably empty. Then he became aware that the planks of the middle decking were dotted with moving black specks.

His attention was riveted by these specks. They were all walking in directions radiating from the fallen man in a manner—the image came unsought to his mind—like the crowd dispersing from a bull-fight.

He became aware of Gerilleau beside him. "Capo," he said, "have you your glasses? Can you focus as closely as those planks there?"

Gerilleau made an effort, grunted, and handed him the glasses.

There followed a moment of scrutiny. "It's ants," said the Englishman, and handed the focused field-glasses back to Gerilleau.

His impression of them was of a crowd of large black ants, very like ordinary ants except for their size, and for the fact that some of the larger of them bore a sort of clothing of grey. But at the time his inspection was too brief for particulars. The head of Lieutenant da Cunha appeared over the side of the cuberta, and a brief colloquy ensued.

"You must go aboard," said Gerilleau.

The lieutenant objected that the boat was full of ants.

"You have your boots," said Gerilleau.

The lieutenant changed the subject. "How did these men die?" he asked.

Captain Gerilleau embarked upon speculations that Holroyd could not follow, and the two men disputed with a certain increasing vehemence. Holroyd took up the field-glass and resumed his scrutiny, first of the ants and then of the dead man amidships.

He has described these ants to me very particularly.

He says they were as large as any ants he has ever seen, black and moving with a steady deliberation very different from the mechanical fussiness of the common ant. About one in twenty was much larger than its fellows, and with an exceptionally large head. These reminded him at once of the master workers who are said to rule over the leaf-cutter ants; like them they seemed to be directing and co-ordinating the general movements. They tilted their bodies back in a manner altogether singular as if they made some use of the fore feet. And he had a curious fancy that he was too far off to verify, that most of these ants of both kinds were wearing accoutrements, had things strapped about their bodies by bright white bands like white metal threads. . . .

He put down the glasses abruptly, realising that the question of discipline between the captain and his subordinate had become acute.

"It is your duty," said the captain, "to go aboard. It is my instructions."

The lieutenant seemed on the verge of refusing. The head of one of the mulatto sailors appeared beside him.

"I believe these men were killed by the ants," said Holroyd abruptly in English.

The captain burst into a rage. He made no answer to Holroyd. "I have commanded you to go aboard," he screamed to his subordinate in Portuguese. "If you do not go aboard forthwith it is mutiny—rank mutiny. Mutiny and cowardice! Where is the courage that should animate us? I will have you in irons, I will have you shot like a dog."

He began a torrent of abuse and curses, he danced to and fro. He shook his fists, he behaved as if beside himself with rage, and the lieutenant, white and still, stood looking at him. The crew appeared forward, with amazed faces.

Suddenly, in a pause of this outbreak, the lieutenant came to some heroic decision, saluted, drew himself together and clambered upon the deck of the cuberta.

"Ah!" said Gerilleau, and his mouth shut like a trap. Holroyd saw the ants retreating before da Cunha's boots. The Portuguese walked slowly to the fallen man, stooped down, hesitated, clutched his coat and turned him over. A black swarm of ants rushed out of the clothes, and da Cunha stepped back very quickly and trod two or three times on the deck.

Holroyd put up the glasses. He saw the scattered ants about the invader's feet, and doing what he had never seen ants doing before. They had nothing of the blind movements of the common ant; they were looking at him—as a rallying crowd of men might look at some gigantic monster that had dispersed it.

"How did he die?" the captain shouted.

Holroyd understood the Portuguese to say the body was too much eaten to tell.

" What is there forward? " asked Gerilleau.

The lieutenant walked a few paces, and began his answer in Portuguese. He stopped abruptly and beat off something from his leg. He made some peculiar steps as if he was trying to stamp on something invisible, and went quickly towards the side. Then he controlled himself, turned about, walked deliberately forward to the hold, clambered up to the fore decking, from which the sweeps are worked, stooped for a time over the second man, groaned audibly, and made his way back and aft to the cabin, moving very rigidly. He turned and began a conversation with his captain, cold and respectful in tone on either side, contrasting vividly with the wrath and insult of a few moments before. Holroyd gathered only fragments of its purport.

He reverted to the field-glass, and was surprised to find the ants had vanished from all the exposed surfaces of the deck. He turned towards the shadows beneath the decking, and it seemed to him they were full of watching eyes.

The cuberta, it was agreed, was derelict, but too full of ants to put men aboard to sit and sleep: it must be towed. The lieutenant went forward to take in and adjust the cable, and the men in the boat stood up to be ready to help him. Holroyd's glasses searched the canoe.

He became more and more impressed by the fact that a great if minute and furtive activity was going on. He perceived that a number of gigantic ants— they seemed nearly a couple of inches in length— carrying oddly-shaped burthens for which he could imagine no use—were moving in rushes from one point of obscurity to another. They did not move in columns across the exposed places, but in open, spaced-out lines, oddly suggestive of the rushes of modern infantry advancing under fire. A number were taking cover under the dead man's clothes, and a perfect swarm was gathering along the side over which da Cunha must presently go.

He did not see them actually rush for the lieutenant as he returned, but he has no doubt they did make a concerted rush. Suddenly the lieutenant was shouting and cursing and beating at his legs. " I'm stung! " he shouted, with a face of hate and accusation towards Gerilleau.

Then he vanished over the side, dropped into his boat, and plunged at once into the water. Holroyd heard the splash.

The three men in the boat pulled him out and brought him aboard, and that night he died.

3

Holroyd and the captain came out of the cabin in which the swollen and contorted body of the lieutenant lay and stood together at the stern of the monitor, staring at the sinsister vessel they trailed behind them. It was a close, dark night that had only phantom flickerings of sheet lightning to illuminate it. The cuberta, a vague black triangle, rocked about in the steamer's wake, her sails bobbing and flapping, and the black smoke from the funnels, spark-lit ever and again, streamed over her swaying masts.

Gerilleau's mind was inclined to run on the unkind things the lieutenant had said in the heat of his last fever.

" He says I murdered 'im," he protested. " It is simply absurd. Some one 'ad to go aboard. Are we to run away from these confounded ants whenever they show up? "

Holroyd said nothing. He was thinking of a disciplined rush of little black shapes across bare sunlit planking.

"It was his place to go," harped Gerilleau. "He died in the execution of his duty. What has he to complain of? Murdered! . . . But the poor fellow was—what is it?—demented. He was not in his right mind. The poison swelled him. . . . U'm."

They came to a long silence.

"We will sink that canoe—burn it."

"And then?"

The inquiry irritated Gerilleau. His shoulders went up, his hands flew out at right angles from his body. "What is one to *do*?" he said, his voice going up to an angry squeak.

"Anyhow," he broke in vindictively, "every ant in dat cuberta!—I will burn dem alive!"

Holroyd was not moved to conversation. A distant ululation of howling monkeys filled the sultry night with foreboding sounds, and as the gunboat drew near the black mysterious banks this was reinforced by a depressing clamour of frogs.

"What is one to *do*?" the captain repeated after a vast interval, and suddenly becoming active and savage and blasphemous, decided to burn the *Santa Rosa* without further delay. Every one aboard was pleased by that idea every one helped with zest; they pulled in the cable, cut it, and dropped the boat and fired her with tow and kerosene, and soon the cuberta was crackling and flaring merrily amidst the immensities of the tropical night. Holroyd watched the mounting yellow flare against the blackness, and the livid flashes of sheet lightning that came and went above the forest summits, throwing them into momentary silhouette, and his stoker stood behind him watching also.

The stoker was stirred to the depths of his linguistics. "*Saüba* go pop, pop," he said, "Wahaw!" and laughed richly.

But Holroyd was thinking that these little creatures on the decked canoe had also eyes and brains.

84

The whole thing impressed him as incredibly foolish and wrong, but—what was one to *do*? This question came back enormously reinforced on the morrow, when at last the gunboat reached Badama.

This place, with its leaf-thatch-covered houses and sheds, its creeper-invaded sugar-mill, its little jetty of timber and canes, was very still in the morning heat, and showed never a sign of living men. Whatever ants there were at that distance were too small to see.

" All the people have gone," said Gerilleau, " but we will do one thing anyhow. We will 'oot and vissel."

So Holroyd hooted and whistled.

Then the captain fell into a doubting fit of the worst kind. " Dere is one thing we can do," he said presently.

" What's that? " said Holroyd.

" 'Oot and vissel again."

So they did.

The captain walked his deck and gesticulated to himself. He seemed to have many things on his mind. Fragments of speeches came from his lips. He appeared to be addressing some imaginary public tribunal either in Spanish or Portuguese. Holroyd's improving ear detected something about ammunition. He came out of these preoccupations suddenly into English. " My dear 'Olroyd! " he cried, and broke off with " But what *can* one do? "

They took the boat and the field-glasses, and went close in to examine the place. They made out a number of big ants, whose still postures had a certain effect of watching them, dotted about the edge of the rude embarkation jetty. Gerilleau tried ineffectual pistol shots at these. Holroyd thinks he distinguished curious earthworks running between the nearer houses, that may have been the work of the insect conquerors of those human habitations. The explorers pulled past the jetty, and became aware of a human skeleton wearing a loin cloth, and very bright and clean and shining, lying beyond. They came to a pause regarding this. . . .

"I 'ave all dose lives to consider," said Gerilleau suddenly.

Holroyd turned and stared at the captain, realising slowly that he referred to the unappetising mixture of races that constituted his crew.

"To send a landing party—it is impossible— impossible. They will be poisoned, they will swell, they will swell up and abuse me and die. It is totally impossible. . . . If we land, I must land alone, alone, in thick boots and with my life in my hand. Perhaps I should live. Or again—I might not land. I do not know. I do not know."

Holroyd thought he did, but he said nothing.

"De whole thing," said Gerilleau suddenly, "'as been got up to make me ridiculous. De whole thing!"

They paddled about and regarded the clean white skeleton from various points of view, and then they returned to the gunboat. Then Gerilleau's indecisions became terrible. Steam was got up, and in the afternoon the monitor went on up the river with an air of going to ask somebody something, and by sunset came back again and anchored. A thunderstorm gathered and broke furiously, and then the night became beautifully cool and quiet and every one slept on deck. Except Gerilleau, who tossed about and muttered. In the dawn he awakened Holroyd.

"Lord!" said Holroyd, "what now?"

"I have decided," said the captain.

"What—to land?" said Holroyd, sitting up brightly.

"No!" said the captain, and was for a time very reserved. "I have decided," he repeated, and Holroyd manifested symptoms of impatience.

"Well—yes," said the captain, "*I shall fire de big gun!*"

And he did! Heaven knows what the ants thought

of it, but he did. He fired it twice with great sternness and ceremony. All the crew had wadding in their ears, and there was an effect of going into action about the whole affair, and first they hit and wrecked the old sugar-mill, and then they smashed the abandoned store behind the jetty. And then Gerilleau experienced the inevitable reaction.

"It is no good," he said to Holroyd; "no good at all. No sort of bally good. We must go back—for instructions. Dere will be de devil of a row about dis ammunition—oh! de *devil* of a row! You don't know, 'Olroyd. . . ."

He stood regarding the world in infinite perplexity for a space.

"But what else was there to *do*?" he cried.

In the afternoon the monitor started down-stream again, and in the evening a landing party took the body of the lieutenant and buried it on the bank upon which the new ants have so far not appeared. . . .

4

I heard this story in a fragmentary state from Holroyd not three weeks ago.

These new ants have got into his brain, and he has come back to England with the idea, as he says, of "exciting people" about them "before it is too late." He said they threaten British Guiana, which cannot be much over a trifle of a thousand miles from their present sphere of activity, and that the Colonial Office ought to get to work upon them at once. He declaims with great passion: "These are intelligent ants. Just think what that means!"

There can be no doubt they are a serious pest, and that the Brazilian Government is well advised in offering a prize of five hundred pounds for some effectual method of extirpation. It is certain too that since they first appeared in the hills beyond Badama, about three years ago, they have achieved extraordinary conquests. The whole of the south bank of the Batemo River, for nearly sixty miles, they have in their effectual occupation; they have driven men out completely, occupied plantations and settlements, and boarded and captured at least one ship. It is even said they have in some inexplicable way bridged the very considerable Capuarana arm and pushed many miles towards the Amazon itself. There can be little doubt that they are far more reasonable and with a far better social organisation than any previously known ant species; instead of being in dispersed societies they are organised into what is in effect a single nation; but their peculiar and immediate formidableness lies not so much in this as in the intelligent use they make of poison against their larger enemies. It would seem this poison of theirs is closely akin to snake poison, and it is highly probable they actually manufacture it, and that the larger individuals among them carry the needle-like crystals of it in their attacks upon men.

Of course, it is extremely difficult to get any detailed information about these new competitors for the sovereignty of the globe. No eye-witnesses of their activity, except for such glimpses as Holroyd's, have survived the encounter. The most extraordinary legends of their prowess and capacity are in circulation in the region of the Upper Amazon, and grow daily as the steady advance of the invader stimulates men's imaginations through their fears. These strange little creatures are credited not only with the use of implements and a knowledge of fire and metals and with organised feats of engineering that stagger our northern minds—unused as we are to such feats as that of the Saubas of Rio de Janeiro, who in 1841 drove a tunnel under the Parahyba where it is as wide as the Thames at London Bridge—but with an organised and detailed method of record and communication analogous to our books. So far their action has been a steady progressive settlement, involving the flight or slaughter of every human being in the new areas they invade. They are increasing rapidly in numbers, and Holroyd at least is firmly convinced that they will finally dispossess man over the whole of tropical South America.

And why should they stop at tropical South America?

Well, there they are, anyhow. By 1911 or thereabouts, if they go on as they are doing, they ought to strike the Capuarana Extension Railway, and force themselves upon the attention of the European capitalist.

By 1920 they will be half-way down the Amazon. I fix 1950 or '60 at the latest for the discovery of Europe.

THE MOTH

PROBABLY YOU have heard of Hapley—not W. T. Hapley, the son, but the celebrated Hapley, the Hapley of *Periplaneta Hapliia*, Hapley the entomologist.

If so you know at least of the great feud between Hapley and Professor Pawkins, though certain of its consequences may be new to you. For those who have not, a word or two of explanation is necessary, which the idle reader may go over with a glancing eye, if his indolence so incline him.

It is amazing how very widely diffused is the ignorance of such really important matters as this Hapley-Pawkins feud. Those epoch-making controversies, again, that have convulsed the Geological Society are, I verily believe, almost entirely unknown outside the fellowship of that body. I have heard men of fair general education, even refer to the great scenes at these meetings as vestry-meeting squabbles. Yet the great hate of the English and Scotch geologists has lasted now half a century, and has " left deep and abundant marks upon the body of the science." And this Hapley-Pawkins business, though perhaps a more personal affair, stirred passions as profound, if not profounder. Your common man has no conception of the zeal that animates a scientific investigator, the fury of contradiction you can arouse in him. It is the *odium theologicum* in a new form. There are men, for instance, who would gladly burn Professor Ray Lankester at Smithfield for his treatment of the Mollusca in the Encyclopaedia. That fantastic extension of the Cephalopods to cover the Pteropods . . . But I wander from Hapley and Pawkins.

It began years and years ago, with a revision of the Microlepidoptera (whatever these may be) by Pawkins, in which he extinguished a new species created by Hapley. Hapley, who was always quarrelsome, replied by a stinging impeachment of the entire classification of Pawkins.[1] Paw-

[1] " Remarks on Recent Revision of Microlepidoptera." *Quart. Journ. Entomological Soc.*, 1863.

kins in his "Rejoinder" [1] suggested that Hapley's microscope was as defective as his power of observation, and called him an " irresponsible meddler "—Hapley was not a professor at that time. Hapley in his retort,[2] spoke of " blundering collectors " and described, as if inadvertantly, Pawkins' revision as a " miracle of ineptitude." It was war to the knife. However, it would scarcely interest the reader to detail how these two great men quarrelled, and how the split between them widened until from the Microlepidop-tera they were at war upon every open question in ento-mology. There were memorable occasions. At times the Royal Entomological Society meetings resembled nothing so much as the Chamber of Deputies. On the whole, I fancy Pawkins was nearer the truth than Hapley. But Hapley was skilful with his rhetoric, had a turn for ridicule rare in a scientific man, was endowed with vast energy, and had a fine sense of injury in the matter of the extinguished species ; while Pawkins was a man of dull presence, prosy of speech, in shape not unlike a water-barrel, over con-scientious with testimonials, and suspected of jobbing museum appointments. So the young men gathered round Hapley and applauded him. It was a long struggle, vicious from the beginning and growing at last to pitiless antagon-ism. The successive turns of fortune, now an advantage to one side and now to another—now Hapley tormented by some success of Pawkins, and now Pawkins outshone by Hapley, belong rather to the history of entomology than to this story.

But in 1891 Pawkins, whose health had been bad for some time, published some work upon the " mesoblast " of the Death's Head Moth. What the mesoblast of the Death's Head Moth may be does not matter a rap in this story. But the work was far below his usual standard and gave Hapley an opening he had coveted for years. He must have worked night and day to make the most of his advantage.

In an elaborate critique he rent Pawkins to tatters—one can fancy the man's disordered black hair, and his queer

[1] " Rejoinder to certain Remarks," etc. *Ibid.* 1864.
[2] " Further Remarks," etc. *Ibid.*

dark eyes flashing as he went for his antagonist—and Pawkins made a reply, halting, ineffectual, with painful gaps of silence, and yet malignant. There was no mistaking his will to wound Hapley, nor his incapacity to do it. But few of those who heard him—I was absent from that meeting—realised how ill the man was.

Hapley got his opponent down, and meant to finish him. He followed with a simply brutal attack upon Pawkins, in the form of a paper upon the development of moths in general, a paper showing evidence of a most extraordinary amount of mental labour, and yet couched in a violently controversial tone. Violent as it was, an editorial note witnesses that it was modified. It must have covered Pawkins with shame and confusion of face. It left no loophole ; it was murderous in argument, and utterly contemptuous in tone ; an awful thing for the declining years of a man's career.

The world of entomologists waited breathlessly for the rejoinder from Pawkins. He would try one, for Pawkins had always been game. But when it came it surprised them. For the rejoinder of Pawkins was to catch influenza, proceed to pneumonia, and die.

It was perhaps as effectual a reply as he could make under the circumstances, and largely turned the current of feeling against Hapley. The very people who had most gleefully cheered on those gladiators became serious at the consequence. There could be no reasonable doubt the fret of the defeat had contributed to the death of Pawkins. There was a limit even to scientific controversy, said serious people. Another crushing attack was already in the Press and appeared on the day before the funeral. I don't think Hapley exerted himself to stop it. People remembered how Hapley had hounded down his rival, and forgot that rival's defects. Scathing satire reads ill over fresh mould. The thing provoked comment in the daily papers. This it was that made me think that you had probably heard of Hapley and this controversy. But, as I have already remarked, scientific workers live very much in a world of their own ; half the people, I dare say, who go along Piccadilly to the Academy every year, could not tell you where the learned societies abide. Many even think that research is a kind of happy-family cage in which all kinds of men lie down together in peace.

In his private thoughts Hapley could not forgive Pawkins for dying. In the first place, it was a mean dodge to escape the absolute pulverisation Hapley had in hand for him, and in the second, it left Hapley's mind with a queer gap in it. For twenty years he had worked hard, sometimes far into the night, and seven days a week, with microscope, scalpel, collecting-net, and pen, and almost entirely with reference to Pawkins. The European reputation he had won had come as an incident in that great antipathy. He had gradually worked up to a climax in this last controversy. It had killed Pawkins, but it had also thrown Hapley out of gear, so to speak, and his doctor advised him to give up work for a time, and rest. So Hapley went down into a quiet village in Kent, and thought day and night of Pawkins, and good things it was now impossible to say about him.

At last Hapley began to realise in what direction the pre-occupation tended. He determined to make a fight for it, and started by trying to read novels. But he could not get his mind off Pawkins, white in the face and making his last speech—every sentence a beautiful opening for Hapley. He turned to fiction—and found it had no grip on him. He read the *Island Nights' Entertainments* until his sense of causation was shocked beyond endurance by the Bottle Imp. Then he went to Kipling, and found he "proved nothing" besides being irreverent and vulgar. These scientific people have their limitations. Then, unhappily, he tried Besant's *Inner House*, and the opening chapter set his mind upon learned societies and Pawkins at once.

So Hapley turned to chess, and found it a little more soothing. He soon mastered the moves and the chief gambits and commoner closing positions, and began to beat the Vivar. But then the cylindrical contours of the opposite king began to resemble Pawkins standing up and gasping ineffectually against check-mate, and Hapley decided to give up chess.

Perhaps the study of some new branch of science would after all be better diversion. The best rest is change of occupation. Hapley determined to plunge at diatoms, and had one of his smaller microscopes and Halibut's monograph sent down from London. He thought that perhaps if he could get up a vigorous quarrel with Halibut, he might be able to begin life afresh and forget Pawkins. And very soon he was hard at work in his habitual strenuous fashion, at these microscopic denizens of the wayside pool.

It was on the third day of the diatoms that Hapley became aware of a novel addition to the local fauna. He was working late at the microscope, and the only light in the room was the brilliant little lamp with the special form of green shade. Like all experienced microscopists, he kept both eyes open. It is the only way to avoid excessive fatigue. One eye was over the instrument, and bright and distinct before that was the circular field of the microscope, across which a brown diatom was slowly moving. With the other eye Hapley saw, as it were, without seeing. He was only dimly conscious of the brass side of the instrument, the illuminated part of the table-cloth, a sheet of note-paper, the foot of the lamp, and the darkened room beyond.

Suddenly his attention drifted from one eye to the other. The table-cloth was of the material called tapestry by shopmen, and rather brightly coloured. The pattern was in gold, with a small amount of crimson and pale blue upon a grayish ground. At one point the pattern seemed displaced, and there was a vibrating movement of the colours at this point.

Hapley suddenly moved his head back and looked with both eyes. His mouth fell open with astonishment.

It was a large moth or butterfly ; its wings spread in butterfly fashion !

It was strange it should be in the room at all, for the windows were closed. Strange that it should not have attracted his attention when fluttering to its present position. Strange that it should match the tablecloth. Stranger far that to him, Hapley, the great entomologist, it was altogether unknown. There was no delusion. It was crawling slowly towards the foot of the lamp.

"New Genus, by heavens! And in England!" said Hapley, staring.

Then he suddenly thought of Pawkins. Nothing would have maddened Pawkins more. . . . And Pawkins was dead!

Something about the head and body of the insect became singularly suggestive of Pawkins, just as the chess king had been.

"Confound Pawkins!" said Hapley. "But I must catch this." And looking around him for some means of capturing the moth, he rose slowly out of his chair. Suddenly the insect rose, struck the edge of the lampshade— Hapley heard the "ping"—and vanished into the shadow.

In a moment Hapley had whipped off the shade, so that the whole room was illuminated. The thing had disappeared, but soon his practised eye detected it upon the wall-paper near the door. He went towards it poising the lamp-shade for capture.

Before he was within striking distance, however, it had risen and was fluttering round the room. After the fashion of its kind, it flew with sudden starts and turns, seeming to vanish here and reappear there. Once Hapley struck, and missed ; then again.

The third time he hit his microscope. The instrument swayed, struck and overturned the lamp, and fell noisily upon the floor. The lamp turned over on the table and, very luckily, went out. Hapley was left in the dark. With a start he felt the strange moth blunder into his face.

It was maddening. He had no lights. If he opened the door of the room the thing would get away. In the darkness he saw Pawkins quite distinctly laughing at him. Pawkins had ever an oily laugh. He swore furiously and stamped his foot on the floor.

There was a timid rapping at the door.

Then it opened, perhaps a foot, and very slowly. The alarmed face of the landlady appeared behind a pink candle flame ; she wore a night-cap over her gray hair and had some purple garment over her shoulders. "What *was* that fearful smash?" she said. "Has anything——"
The strange moth appeared fluttering about the chink of

the door. " Shut that door ! " said Hapley, and suddenly rushed at her.

The door slammed hastily. Hapley was left alone in the dark. Then, in the pause, he heard his landlady scuttle upstairs, lock her door, and drag something heavy across the room and put against it.

It became evident to Hapley that his conduct and appearance had been strange and alarming. Confound the moth ! and Pawkins ! However, it was a pity to lose the moth now. He felt his way into the hall and found the matches, after sending his hat down upon the floor with a noise like a drum. With the lighted candle he returned to the sitting-room. No moth was to be seen. Yet once for a moment it seemed that the thing was fluttering round his head. Hapley very suddenly decided to give up the moth and go to bed. But he was excited. All night long his sleep was broken by dreams of the moth, Pawkins, and his landlady. Twice in the night he turned out and soused his head in cold water.

One thing was very clear to him. His landlady could not possibly understand about the strange moth, especially as he had failed to catch it. No one but an entomologist would understand quite how he felt. She was probably frightened at his behaviour, and yet he failed to see how he could explain it. He decided to say nothing further about the events of last night. After breakfast he saw her in her garden, and decided to go out and talk to reassure her. He talked to her about beans and potatoes, bees, caterpillars, and the price of fruit. She replied in her usual manner, but she looked at him a little suspiciously, and kept walking as he walked, so that there was always a bed of flowers, or a row of beans, or something of the sort, between them. After a while he began to feel singularly irritated at this, and to conceal his vexation went indoors and presently went out for a walk.

The moth, or butterfly, trailing an odd flavour of Pawkins with it, kept coming into that walk, though he did his best to keep his mind off it. Once he saw it quite distinctly, with its wings flattened out, upon the old stone wall that runs along the west edge of the park, but going up to it he found it was only two lumps of gray and yellow lichen. " That," said Hapley, " is the reverse of mimicry. Instead of a butterfly looking like a stone, here is a stone looking like a butterfly ! " Once something hovered and fluttered round his head, but by an effort of will he drove that impression out of his mind again.

In the afternoon Hapley called upon the Vicar, and argued with him upon theological questions. They sat in the little arbour covered with brier, and smoked as they wrangled. " Look at that moth ! " said Hapley, suddenly, pointing to the edge of the wooden table.

" Where ? " said the Vicar.

" You don't see a moth on the edge of the table there ? " said Hapley.

" Certainly not," said the Vicar.

Hapley was thunderstruck. He gasped. The Vicar was staring at him. Clearly the man saw nothing. " The eye of faith is no better than the eye of science," said Hapley awkwardly.

" I don't see your point," said the Vicar, thinking it was part of the argument.

That night Hapley found the moth crawling over his counterpane. He sat on the edge of the bed in his shirt sleeves and reasoned with himself. Was it pure hallucination ? He knew he was slipping, and he battled for his sanity with the same silent energy he had formerly displayed against Pawkins. So persistent is mental habit, that he felt as if it were still a struggle with Pawkins. He was well versed in psychology. He knew that such visual illusions do come as a result of mental strain. But the point was, he did not only *see* the moth, he had heard it when it touched the edge of the lampshade, and afterwards when it hit against the wall, and he had felt it strike his face in the dark.

He looked at it. It was not at all dreamlike, but perfectly clear and solid-looking in the candle-light. He saw the hairy body, and the short feathery antennae, the jointed legs, even a place where the down was rubbed from the wing He suddenly felt angry with himself for being afraid of a little insect.

His landlady had got the servant to sleep with her that night, because she was afraid to be alone. In addition she had locked the door, and put the chest of drawers against it. They listened and talked in whispers after they had gone to bed, but nothing occurred to alarm them. About eleven they had ventured to put the candle out, and had both dozed off to sleep. They woke up with a start, and sat up in bed, listening in the darkness.

Then they heard slippered feet going to and fro in Hapley's room. A chair was overturned, and there was a violent dab at the wall. Then a china mantel ornament smashed upon the fender. Suddenly the door of the room opened, and they heard him upon the landing. They clung to one another, listening. He seemed to be dancing upon the staircase. Now he would go down three or four steps quickly, then up again, then hurry down into the hall. They heard the umbrella stand go over, and the fanlight break. Then the bolt shot and the chain rattled. He was opening the door.

They hurried to the window. It was a dim gray night ; an almost unbroken sheet of watery cloud was sweeping across the moon, and the hedge and trees in front of the house were black against the pale roadway. They saw Hapley, looking like a ghost in his shirt and white trousers, running to and fro in the road, and beating the air. Now he would stop, now he would dart very rapidly at something invisible, now he would move upon it with stealthy strides. At last he went out of sight up the road towards the down. Then, while they argued who should go down and lock the door, he returned. He was walking very fast, and he came straight into the house, closed the door carefully, and went quietly up to his bedroom. Then everything was silent.

" Mrs. Colville," said Hapley, calling down the staircase next morning, " I hope I did not alarm you last night."

" You may well ask that ! " said Mrs. Colville.

" The fact is, I am a sleep-walker, and the last two nights I have been without my sleeping mixture. There is nothing to be alarmed about, really. I am sorry I made such an ass of myself. I will go over the down to Shoreham, and get some stuff to make me sleep soundly. I ought to have done that yesterday."

But half-way over the down, by the chalk pits, the moth came upon Hapley again. He went on, trying to keep his mind upon chess problems, but it was no good. The thing fluttered into his face, and he struck at it with his hat in self-defence. Then rage, the old rage—the rage he had so often felt against Pawkins—came upon him again. He went on, leaping and striking at the eddying insect. Suddenly he trod on nothing, and fell headlong.

There was a gap in his sensations, and Hapley found himself sitting on the heap of flints in front of the opening of the chalk-pits, with a leg twisted back under him. The strange moth was still fluttering round his head. He struck at it with his hand, and turning his head saw two men approaching him. One was the village doctor. It occurred to Hapley that this was lucky. Then it came into his mind with extraordinary vividness, that no one would ever be able to see the strange moth except himself, and that it behoved him to keep silent about it.

Late that night, however, after his broken leg was set, he was feverish and forgot his self-restraint. He was lying flat on his bed, and he began to run his eyes round the room to see if the moth was still about. He tried not to do this, but it was no good.

He soon caught sight of the thing resting close to his hand, by the night-light, on the green table-cloth. The wings quivered. With a sudden wave of anger he smote at it with his fist, and the nurse woke up with a shriek. He had missed it.

"That moth!" he said; and then, "It was fancy. Nothing!"

All the time he could see quite clearly the insect going round the cornice and darting across the room, and he could also see that the nurse saw nothing of it and looked at him strangely. He must keep himself in hand. He knew he was a lost man if he did not keep himself in hand. But as the night waned the fever grew upon him, and the very dread he had of seeing the moth made him see it. About five, just as the dawn was gray, he tried to get out of bed and catch it, though his leg was afire with pain. The nurse had to struggle with him.

On account of this, they tied him down to the bed. At this the moth grew bolder, and once he felt it settle in his hair. Then, because he struck out violently with his arms, they tied these also. At this the moth came and crawled over his face, and Hapley wept, swore, screamed, prayed for them to take it off him, unavailingly.

The doctor was a blockhead, a just-qualified general practioner, and quite ignorant of mental science. He simply said there was no moth. Had he possessed the wit, he might still, perhaps, have saved Hapley from his fate by entering into his delusion, and covering his face with gauze, as he prayed might be done. But, as I say, the doctor was a blockhead, and until the leg was healed Hapley was kept tied to his bed, and with the imaginary moth crawling over him. It never left him while he was awake and it grew to a monster in his dreams. While he was awake he longed for sleep, and from sleep he awoke screaming.

So now Hapley is spending the remainder of his days in a padded room, worried by a moth that no one else can see. The asylum docotr calls it hallucination ; but Hapley, when he is in his easier mood, and can talk, says it is the ghost of Pawkins, and consequently a unique specimen and well worth the trouble of catching.

THE STORY OF THE LATE
MR ELVESHAM.

I SET this story down, not expecting it will be believed, but if possible, to prepare a way of escape for the next victim. He, perhaps, may profit by my misfortune. My own case, I know, is hopeless, and I am now in some measure prepared to meet my fate.

My name is Edward George Eden. I was born at Trentham, in Staffordshire, my father being employed in the gardens there. I lost my mother when I was three years old, and my father when I was five, my uncle, George Eden, then adopting me as his own son. He was a single man, self-educated, and well-known in Birmingham as an enterprising journalist ; he educated me generously, fired my ambition to succeed in the world, and at his death, which happened four years ago, left me his entire fortune, a matter of about five hundred pounds after all outgoing charges were paid. I was then eighteen. He advised me in his will to expend the money in completing my education. I had already chosen the profession of medicine, and through his posthumous generosity and my good fortune in a scholarship competition, I became a medical student at University College, London. At the time of the beginning of my story I lodged at 11A University Street in a little upper room, very shabbily furnished and draughty, over-looking the back of Shoolbred's premises. I used this little room both to live in and sleep in, because I was anxious to eke out my means to the very last shillingsworth.

I was taking a pair of shoes to be mended at a shop in the Tottenham Court Road when I first encountered the little old man with the yellow face, with whom my life has now become so inextricably entangled. He was standing on the kerb, and staring at the number on the door in a doubtful way, as I opened it. His eyes—they were dull gray eyes, and reddish under the rims—fell

to my face, and his countenance immediately assumed
an expression of corrugated amiability.

"You come," he said, "apt to the moment. I had
forgotten the number of your house. How do you do,
Mr. Eden?"

I was a little astonished at his familiar address, for I
had never set eyes on the man before. I was a little annoyed,
too, at his catching me with my boots under my arm. He
noticed my lack of cordiality.

"Wonder who the deuce I am, eh? A friend, let me
assure you. I have seen you before, though you haven't
seen me. Is there anywhere where I can talk to you?"

I hesitated. The shabbiness of my room upstairs was
not a matter for every stranger. "Perhaps," said I, "we
might walk down the street. I'm unfortunately prevented
——" My gesture explained the sentence before I had
spoken it.

"The very thing," he said, and faced this way, and then
that. "The street? Which way shall we go?" I slipped
my boots down in the passage. "Look here!" he said
abruptly; "this business of mine is a rigmarole. Come
and lunch with me, Mr. Eden. I'm an old man, a very old
man, and not good at explanations, and what with my
piping voice and the clatter of the traffic——"

He laid a persuasive skinny hand that trembled a little
upon my arm.

I was not so old that an old man might not treat me to a
lunch. Yet at the same time I was not altogether pleased by
this abrupt invitation. "I had rather——" I began.
"But I had rather," he said, catching me up, "and a
certain civility is surely due to my gray hairs."

And so I consented, and went with him.

He took me to Blavitiski's; I had to walk slowly to
accommodate myself to his paces; and over such a lunch
as I had never tasted before, he fended off my leading
question, and I took a better note of his appearance. His
clean-shaven face was lean and wrinkled, his shrivelled
lips fell over a set of false teeth, and his white hair was thin
and rather long; he seemed small to me—though indeed,
most people seemed small to me—and his shoulders were

rounded and bent. And watching him, I could not help but observe that he too was taking note of me, running his eyes, with a curious touch of greed in them, over me, from my broad shoulders to my sun-tanned hands, and up to my freckled face again. "And now," said he, as we lit our cigarettes, "I must tell you of the business in hand.

"I must tell you, then, that I am an old man, a very old man." He paused momentarily. "And it happens that I have money that I must presently be leaving, and never a child have I to leave it to." I thought of the confidence trick, and resolved I would be on the alert for the vestiges of my five hundred pounds. He proceeded to enlarge on his loneliness, and the trouble he had to find a proper disposition of his money. "I have weighed this plan and that plan, charities, institutions, and scholarships, and libraries, and I have come to this conclusion at last,"—he fixed his eyes on my face—"that I will find some young fellow, ambitious, pure-minded, and poor, healthy in body and healthy in mind, and, in short, make him my heir, give him all that I have." He repeated, "Give him all that I have. So that he will suddenly be lifted out of all the trouble and struggle in which his sympathies have been educated, to freedom and influence."

I tried to seem disinterested. With a transparent hypocrisy I said, "And you want my help, my professional services maybe, to find that person."

He smiled, and looked at me over his cigarette, and I laughed at his quiet exposure of my modest pretence.

"What a career such a man might have!" he said. "It fills me with envy to think how I have accumulated that another man may spend——

"But there are conditions, of course, burdens to be imposed. He must, for instance, take my name. You cannot expect everything without some return. And I must go into all the circumstances of his life before I can accept him. He *must* be sound. I must know his heredity, how his parents and grandparents died, have the strictest inquiries made into his private morals."

This modified my secret congratulations a little.

"And do I understand," said I, "that I——"

"Yes," he said, almost fiercely. "You. *You.*"

I answered never a word. My imagination was dancing wildly, my innate scepticism was useless to modify its transports. There was not a particle of gratitude in my mind—I did not know what to say nor how to say it. "But why me in particular?" I said at last.

He had chanced to hear of me from Professor Haslar, he said, as a typically sound and sane young man, and he wished, as far as possible, to leave his money where health and integrity were assured.

That was my first meeting with the little old man. He was mysterious about himself; he would not give his name yet, he said, and after I had answered some questions of his, he left me at the Blavitiski portal. I noticed that he drew a handful of gold coins from his pocket when it came to paying for the lunch. His insistence upon bodily health was curious. In accordance with an arrangement we had made I applied that day for a life policy in the Loyal Insurance Company for a large sum, and I was exhaustively overhauled by the medical advisers of that company in the subsequent week. Even that did not satisfy him, and he insisted I must be re-examined by the great Doctor Henderson.

It was Friday in Whitsun week before he came to a decision. He called me down, quite late in the evening —nearly nine it was—from cramming chemical equations for my Preliminary Scientific examination. He was standing in the passage under the feeble gas-lamp, and his face was a grotesque interplay of shadows. He seemed more bowed than when I had first seen him, and his cheeks had sunk in a little.

His voice shook with emotion. "Everything is satisfactory, Mr. Eden," he said. "Everything is quite, quite satisfactory. And this night of all nights, you must dine with me and celebrate your—accession." He was interrupted by a cough. "You won't have long to wait, either," he said, wiping his handkerchief across his lips, and gripping my hand with his long bony claw that was disengaged. "Certainly not very long to wait."

We went into the street and called a cab. I remember

every incident of that drive vividly, the swift, easy motion, the vivid contrast of gas and oil and electric light, the crowds of people in the streets, the place in Regent Street to which we went, and the sumptuous dinner we were served with there. I was disconcerted at first by the well-dressed waiter's glances at my rough clothes, bothered by the stones of the olives, but as the champagne warmed my blood, my confidence revived. At first the old man talked of himself. He had already told me his name in the cab ; he was Egbert Elvesham, the great philosopher, whose name I had known since I was a lad at school. It seemed incredible to me that this man, whose intelligence had so early dominated mine, this great abstraction, should suddenly realise itself as this decrepit, familiar figure. I dare say every young fellow who has suddenly fallen among celebrities has felt something of my disappointment. He told me now of the future that the feeble streams of his life would presently leave dry for me, houses, copyrights, investments ; I had never suspected that philosophers were so rich. He watched me drink and eat with a touch of envy. " What a capacity for living you have ! " he said ; and then with a sigh, a sigh of relief I could have thought it, " it will not be long."

" Ay," said I, my head swimming now with champagne ; " I have a future perhaps—of a passing agreeable sort, thanks to you. I shall now have the honour of your name. But you have a past, Such a past as is worth all my future."

He shook his head and smiled, as I thought, with half sad appreciation of my flattering admiration. " That future," he said, " would you in truth change it ? " The waiter came with liqueurs. " You will not perhaps mind taking my name, taking my position, but would you indeed—willingly—take my years ? "

" With your achievements," said I gallantly.

He smiled again. " Kummel—both," he said to the waiter, and turned his attention to a little paper packet he had taken from his pocket. " This hour," said he, " this after-dinner hour is the hour of small things. Here is a scrap of my unpublished wisdom." He opened the packet with his shaking yellow fingers, and showed a little pinkish powder on the paper. "This," said he—"well you must guess what it is. But Kummel—put but a dash of this powder in it—is Himmel."

His large grayish eyes watched mine with an inscrutable expression.

It was a bit of a shock to me to find this great teacher gave his mind to the flavour of liqueurs. However, I feigned an interest in his weakness, for I was drunk enough for such small sycophancy.

He parted the powder between the little glasses, and, rising suddenly, with a strange unexpected dignity, held out his hand towards me. I imitated his action, and the glasses rang. "To a quick succession," said he, and raised his glass towards his lips.

"Not that," I said hastily. "Not that."

He paused with the liqueur at the level of his chin, and his eyes blazing into mine.

"To a long life," said I.

He hesitated. "To a long life," said he, with a sudden bark of laughter, and with eyes fixed on one another we tilted the little glasses. His eyes looked straight into mine, and as I drained the stuff off, I felt a curiously intense sensation. The first touch of it set my brain in a furious tumult; I seemed to feel an actual physical stirring in my skull, and a seething humming filled my ears. I did not notice the flavour in my mouth, the aroma that filled my throat; I saw only the gray intensity of his gaze that burnt into mine. The draught, the mental confusion, the noise and stirring in my head, seemed to last an interminable time. Curious vague impressions of half-forgotten things danced and vanished on the edge of my consciousness. At last he broke the spell. With a sudden explosive sigh he put down his glass.

"Well?" he said.

"It's glorious," said I, though I had not tasted the stuff. My head was spinning. I sat down. My brain was chaos. Then my perception grew clear and minute as though I saw things in a concave mirror. His manner seemed to have changed into something nervous and hasty. He pulled out his watch and grimaced at it.

"Eleven-seven! And to-night I must—Seven twenty-five. Waterloo! I must go at once." He called for the bill, and struggled with his coat. Officious waiters came to our assistance. In another moment I was wishing him good-bye, over the apron of a cab, and still with an absurd feeling of minute distinctness, as though—how can I express it?—I not only saw but *felt* through an inverted opera-glass.

"That stuff," he said. He put his hand to his forehead. "I ought not to have given it to you. It will make your head split to-morrow. Wait a minute. Here." He handed me out a little flat thing like a seidlitz powder. "Take that in water as you are going to bed. The other thing was a drug. Not till you're ready to go to bed, mind. It will clear your head. That's all. Once more shake—Futurus!"

I gripped his shrivelled claw. "Good-bye," he said, and by the droop of his eyelids I judged he too was a little under the influence of that brain-twisting cordial.

He recollected something else with a start, felt in his breast-pocket, and produced another packet, this time a cylinder the size and shape of a shaving-stick. "Here." said he. "I'd almost forgotten. Don't open this until I come to-morrow—but take it now."

It was so heavy that I wellnigh dropped it. "All ri'!" said I, and he grinned at me through the cab window as the cabman flicked his horse into wakefulness. It was a white packet he had given me, with red seals at either end and along its edge. "If this isn't money," said I, "it's platinum or lead."

I stuck it with elaborate care into my pocket, and with a whirling brain walked home through the Regent Street loiterers and the dark back streets beyond Portland Road. I remember the sensations of that walk very vividly, strange as they were. I was still so far myself that I could notice my strange mental state, and wonder whether this stuff I had had was opium—a drug beyond my experience. It is hard now to describe the peculiarity of my mental strangeness—mental doubling vaguely expresses it. As I was walking up Regent Street I found in my mind a queer persuasion that it was Waterloo Station, and had an odd impulse to get into the Polytechnic as a man might get into a train. I put a knuckle in my eye, and it was Regent Street. How can I express it? You see a skilful actor looking quietly at you, he pulls a grimace, and lo!— another person. Is it too extravagant if I tell you that it seemed to me as if Regent Street had, for the moment, done that! Then, being persuaded it was Regent Street again, I was oddly muddled about some fantastic reminiscences that cropped up. "Thirty years ago," thought I, "it was here that I quarrelled with my brother." Then I burst out laughing, to the astonishment and encouragement of a group of night prowlers. Thirty years ago I did not exist, and never in my life had I boasted a brother. The stuff was surely liquid folly, for the poignant regret for that lost brother still clung to me. Along Portland Road the madness took another turn. I began to recall vanished shops, and to compare the street with what it used to be. Confused, troubled thinking is comprehensible enough after the drink I had taken, but what puzzled me were these curiously vivid phantasm memories that had crept into my mind, and not only the memories that had crept in, but also the memories that had slipped out. I stopped opposite Stevens's, the natural history dealers, and cudgelled my brains to think what he had to do with me. A 'bus went by, and sounded exactly like the rumbling of a train. I seemed to be dipping into some dark, remote pit for the recollection. "Of course," said I, at last, "he has promised me three frogs to-morrow. Odd I should have forgotten."

Do they still show children dissolving views? In those I remember one view would begin like a faint ghost, and grow and oust another. In just that way it seemed to me that a ghostly set of new sensations was struggling with those of my ordinary self.

I went on through Euston Road to Tottenham Court Road, puzzled, and a little frightened, and scarcely noticed the unusual way I was taking, for commonly I used to cut through the intervening network of back streets. I turned into University Street, to discover that I had forgotten my number. Only by a strong effort did I recall 11A, and even then it seemed to me that it was a thing some forgotten person had told me. I tried to steady my mind by recalling the incidents of the dinner, and for the life of me I could conjure up no picture of my host's face ; I saw him only as a shadowy outline, as one might see oneself reflected in a window through which one was looking. In his place, however, I had a curious exterior vision of myself, sitting at a table, flushed, bright-eyed, and talkative.

" I must take this other powder," said I. " This is getting impossible."

I tried the wrong side of the hall for my candle and the matches, and had a doubt of which landing my room might be on. " I'm drunk," I said, "that's certain," and blundered needlessly on the staircase to sustain the proposition.

At the first glance my room seemed unfamiliar. ' What rot ! " I said, and stared about me. I seemed to bring myself back by the effort, and the odd phantasmal quality passed into the concrete familiar. There was the old glass still, with my notes on the albumens stuck in the corner of the frame, my old everyday suit of clothes pitched about the floor. And yet it was not so real after all. I felt an idiotic persuasion trying to creep into my mind, as it were, that I was in a railway carriage in a train just stopping, that I was peering out of the window at some unknown station. I gripped the bed-rail firmly to reassure myself. " It's clair-voyance, perhaps," I said. " I must write to the Psychical Research Society."

I put the rouleau on my dressing-table, sat on my bed, and began to take off my boots. It was as if the picture of my present sensations was painted over some other picture that was trying to show through. " Curse it ! " said I ; " my wits are going, or am I in two places at once ? " Half-undressed, I tossed the powder into a glass and drank it off. It effervesced, and became a fluorescent amber colour. Be-for I was in bed my mind was already tranquillised. I felt the pillow at my cheek, and thereupon I must have fallen asleep.

I awoke abruptly out of a dream of strange beasts, and found myself lying on my back. Probably every one knows that dismal, emotional dream from which one escapes,

109

awake indeed, but strangely cowed. There was a curious taste in my mouth, a tired feeling in my limbs, a sense of cutaneous discomfort. I lay with my head motionless on my pillow, expecting that my feeling of strangeness and terror would pass away, and that I should then doze off again to sleep. But instead of that, my uncanny sensations increased. At first I could perceive nothing wrong about me. There was a faint light in the room, so faint that it was the very next thing to darkness, and the furniture stood out in it as vague blots of absolute darkness. I stared with my eyes just over the bedclothes.

It came into my mind that some one had entered the room to rob me of my rouleau of money, but after lying for some moments, breathing regularly to simulate sleep, I realised this was mere fancy. Nevertheless, the uneasy assurance of something wrong kept fast hold of me. With an effort I raised my head from the pillow, and peered about me at the dark. What it was I could not conceive. I looked at the dim shapes around me, the greater and lesser darknesses that indicated curtains, table, fireplace, book-shelves, and so forth. Then I began to perceive something unfamiliar in the forms of the darkness. Had the bed turned round? Yonder should be the bookshelves, and something shrouded and pallid rose there, something that would not answer to the bookshelves, however I looked at it. It was far too big to be my shirt thrown on a chair.

Overcoming a childish terror, I threw back the bedclothes and thrust my leg out of bed. Instead of coming out of my truckle-bed upon the floor, I found my foot scarcely reached the edge of the mattress. I made another step, as it were, and sat up on the edge of the bed. By the side of my bed should be the candle, and the matches upon the broken chair. I put out my hand and touched—nothing. I waved my hand in the darkness, and it came against some heavy hanging, soft and thick in texture, which gave a rustling noise at my touch. I grasped this and pulled it ; it appeared to be a curtain suspended over the head of my bed.

I was now thoroughly awake, and beginning to realise that I was in a strange room. I was puzzled. I tried to recall the overnight circumstances, and I found them now, curiously enough, vivid in my memory : the supper, my reception of the little packages, my wonder whether I was intoxicated, my slow undressing, the coolness to my flushed face of my pillow. I felt a sudden distrust. Was that last night, or the night before ? At any rate, this room was strange to me, and I could not imagine how I had got into it. The dim, pallid outline was growing paler, and I perceived it was a window, with the dark shape of an oval toilet-glass against the weak intimation of the dawn that filtered through the blind. I stood up, and was surprised by a curious feeling of weakness and unsteadiness. With trembling hands outstretched, I walked slowly towards the window, getting, nevertheless, a bruise on the knee from a chair by the way. I fumbled round the glass, which was large, with handsome brass sconces, to find the blind-cord. I could not find any. By chance I took hold of the tassel, and with the click of a spring the blind ran up.

I found myself looking out upon a scene that was altogether strange to me. The night was overcast, and through the flocculent gray of the heaped clouds there filtered a faint half-light of dawn. Just at the edge of the sky the cloud-canopy had a blood-red rim. Below, everything was dark and indistinct, dim hills in the distance, a vague mass of buildings running up into pinnacles, trees like spilt ink, and below the window a tracery of black bushes and pale gray paths. It was so unfamiliar that for the moment I thought myself still dreaming. I felt the toilet-table ; it appeared to be made of some polished wood, and was rather elaborately furnished—there were little cut-glass bottles and a brush upon it. There was also a queer little object, horse-shoe shape it felt, with smooth, hard projections, lying in a saucer. I could find no matches nor candlestick.

I turned my eyes to the room again. Now the blind was up, faint spectres of its furnishing came out of the darkness. There was a huge curtained bed, and the fireplace at its foot had a large white mantel with something of the shimmer of marble.

I leant against the toilet-table, shut my eyes and opened them again, and tried to think. The whole thing was far too real for dreaming. I was inclined to imagine there was still some hiatus in my memory, as a consequence of my draught of that strange liqueur ; that I had come into my inheritance perhaps, and suddenly lost my recollection of everything since my good fortune had been announced. Perhaps if I waited a little, things would be clearer to me again. Yet my dinner with old Elvesham was now singularly vivid and recent. The champagne, the observant waiters, the powder, and the liqueurs—I could have staked my soul it all happened a few hours ago.

And then occurred a thing so trivial and yet so terrible to me that I shiver now to think of that moment. I spoke aloud. I said, "How the devil did I get here ? " . . . *And the voice was not my own.*

It was not my own, it was thin, the articulation was slurred, the resonance of my facial bones was different. Then to reassure myself I ran one hand over the other, and felt loose folds of skin, the bony laxity of age. " Surely," I said, in that horrible voice that had somehow established itself in my throat, " surely this thing is a dream ! " Almost as quickly as if I did it involuntarily, I thrust my fingers into my mouth. My teeth had gone. My finger-tips ran on the flaccid surface of an even row of shrivelled gums. I was sick with dismay and disgust.

I felt then a passionate desire to see myself, to realise at once in its full horror the ghastly change that had come upon me. I tottered to the mantel, and felt along it for matches. As I did so, a barking cough sprang up in my throat, and I clutched the thick flannel nightdress I found about me. There were no matches there, and I suddenly realised that my extremities were cold. Sniffing and coughing, whimpering a little, perhaps, I fumbled back to bed. " It is surely a dream," I whispered to myself as I clambered back, " surely a dream." It was a senile repetition. I pulled the bedclothes over my shoulders, over my ears, I thrust my withered hand under the pillow, and determined to compose myself to sleep. Of course it was a dream. In the morning the dream would be over, and I should wake up strong and vigorous again to my youth and studies. I shut my eyes, breathed regularly, and, finding myself wakeful, began to count slowly through the powers of three.

But the thing I desired would not come. I could not get to sleep. And the persuasion of the inexorable reality of the change that had happened to me grew steadily. Presently I found myself with my eyes wide open, the powers of three forgotten, and my skinny fingers upon my shrivelled gums. I was, indeed, suddenly and abruptly, an old man. I had in some unaccountable manner fallen through my life and come to old age, in some way I had been cheated of all the best of my life, of love, of struggle, of strength, and hope. I grovelled into the pillow and tried to persuade myself that such hallucination was possible. Imperceptibly, steadily, the dawn grew clearer.

At last, despairing of further sleep, I sat up in bed and looked about me. A chill twilight rendered the whole chamber visible. It was spacious and well-furnished, better furnished than any room I had ever slept in before. A candle and matches became dimly visible upon a little pedestal in a recess. I threw back the bedclothes, and, shivering with the rawness of the early morning, albeit it was summer-time, I got out and lit the candle. Then, trembling horribly, so that the extinguisher rattled on its spike—I tottered to the glass and saw—*Elvesham's face*! It was none the less horrible because I had already dimly feared as much. He had already seemed physically weak and pitiful to me, but seen now, dressed only in a coarse flannel nightdress, that fell apart and showed the stringy neck, seen now as my own body, I cannot describe its desolate decrepitude. The hollow cheeks, the straggling tail of dirty gray hair, the rheumy bleared eyes, the quivering, shrivelled lips, the lower displaying a gleam of the pink interior lining, and those horrible dark gums showing. You who are mind and body together, at your natural years, cannot imagine what this fiendish imprisonment meant to me. To be young and full of the desire and energy of youth, and to be caught, and presently to be crushed in this tottering ruin of a body. . . .

But I wander from the course of my story. For some time I must have been stunned at this change that had come upon me. It was daylight when I did so far gather myself together as to think. In some inexplicable way I had been changed, though how, short of magic, the thing had been done, I could not say. And as I thought, the diabolical ingenuity of Elvesham came home to me. It seemed plain to me that as I found myself in his, so he must be in possession of *my* body, of my strength, that is, and my future. But how to prove it? Then, as I thought, the thing became so incredible, even to me, that my mind reeled, and I had to pinch myself, to feel my toothless gums, to see myself in the glass, and touch the things about me, before I could steady myself to face the facts again. Was all life hallucination? Was I indeed Elvesham, and he me? Had I been dreaming of Eden overnight? Was there any Eden? But if I was Elvesham, I should remember where I was on the previous morning, the name of the town in which I lived, what happened before the dream began. I struggled with my thoughts. I recalled the queer doubleness of my memories overnight. But now my mind was clear. Not the ghost of any memories but those proper to Eden could I raise.

" This way lies insanity ! " I cried in my piping voice. I staggered to my feet, dragged my feeble, heavy limbs to the wash-hand stand, and plunged my gray head into a basin of cold water. Then, towelling myself, I tried again. It was no good. I felt beyond all question that I was indeed Eden, not Elvesham. But Eden in Elvesham's body !

Had I been a man of any other age, I might have given myself up to my fate as one enchanted. But in these sceptical days miracles do not pass current. Here was some trick of psychology. What a drug and a steady stare could do, a drug and a steady stare, or some similar treatment, could surely undo. Men have lost their memories before. But to exchange memories as one does umbrellas ! I laughed. Alas, not a healthy laugh, but a wheezing, senile titter. I could have fancied old Elvesham laughing at my plight, and a gust of petulant anger, unusual to me, swept across my feelings. I began dressing eagerly in the clothes I found lying about on the floor, and only realised when I was dressed that it was an evening suit I had assumed. I opened the wardrobe and found some more ordinary clothes, a pair of plaid trousers, and an old-fashioned dressing-gown. I put a venerable smoking-cap on my venerable head, and, coughing a little from my exertions, tottered out upon the landing.

It was then, perhaps, a quarter to six, and the blinds were closely drawn and the house quite silent. The landing was a spacious one, a broad, richly-carpeted staircase went down into the darkness of the hall below, and before me a door ajar showed me a writing-desk, a revolving bookcase, the back of a study chair, and a fine array of bound books, shelf upon shelf.

" My study," I mumbled, and walked across the landing. Then at the sound of my voice a thought struck me, and I went back to the bedroom and put in the set of false teeth. They slipped in with the ease of old habit. " That's better," said I, gnashing them, and so returned to the study.

The drawers of the writing-desk were locked. Its revolving top was also locked. I could see no indications of the keys and there were none in the pockets of my trousers. I shuffled back at once to the bedroom, and went through the dress-suit, and afterwards the pockets of all the garments I could find. I was very eager, and one might have imagined that burglars had been at work, to see my room when I had done. Not only were there no keys to be found, but not a coin, nor a scrap of paper—save only the receipted bill of the overnight dinner.

A curious weariness asserted itself. I sat down and stared at the garments flung here and there, their pockets turned inside out. My first frenzy had already flickered out. Every moment I was beginning to realise the immense intelligence of the plans of my enemy, to see more and more clearly the hopelessness of my position. With an effort I rose and hurried hobbling into the study again. On the staircase was a housemaid pulling up the blinds. She stared, I think, at the expression of my face. I shut the door of the study behind me, and, seizing a poker, began an attack upon the desk. That is how they found me. The cover of the desk was split, the lock smashed, the letters torn out of the pigeon-holes and tossed about the room. In my senile rage I had flung about the pens and other such light stationery, and overturned the ink. Moreover, a large vase upon the mantel had got broken—I do not know how. I could find no cheque-book, no money, no indications of the slightest use for the recovery of my body. I was battering madly at the drawers, when the butler, backed by two women-servants, intruded upon me.

That simply is the story of my change. No one will believe my frantic assertions. I am treated as one demented, and even at this moment I am under restraint. But I am sane, absolutely sane, and to prove it I have sat down to write this story minutely as the things happened to me. I appeal to the reader, whether there is any trace of insanity in the style or method of the story he has been reading. I am a young man locked away in an old man's body. But the clear fact is incredible to every one. Naturally I appear demented to those who will not believe this, naturally I do not know the names of my secretaries, of the doctors who come to see me, of my servants and neighbours, of this town (wherever it is) where I find myself. Naturally I lose myself in my own house, and suffer inconveniences of every sort. Naturally I ask the oddest questions. Naturally I weep and cry out, and have paroxysms of despair. I have no money and no cheque-book. The bank will not recognise my signature, for I suppose that, allowing for the feeble muscles I now have, my hand-writing is still Eden's. These people about me will not let me go to the bank personally. It seems, indeed, that there is no bank in this town, and that I have an account in some part of London. It seems that Elvesham kept the name of his solicitor secret from all his household. I can ascertain nothing. Elvesham was, of course, a profound student of mental science, and all my declarations of the facts of the case merely confirm the theory that my insanity is the outcome of overmuch brood-ing upon psychology. Dreams of the personal identity in-deed! Two days ago I was a healthy youngster, with all life before me ; now I am a furious old man, unkempt, and desperate, and miserable, prowling about a great, luxurious, strange house, watched, feared, and avoided as a lunatic by every one about me. And in London is Elvesham beginning life again in a vigorous body, and with all the accumulated knowledge and wisdom of threescore and ten. He has stolen my life.

What has happened I do not clearly know. In the study are volumes of manuscript notes referring chiefly to the psychology of memory, and parts of what may be either calculations or ciphers in symbols absolutely strange to me. In some passages there are indications that he was also occupied with the philosophy of mathematics. I take it he has transferred the whole of his memories, the accumulation that makes up his personality, from this old withered brain of his to mine, and, similarly, that he has transferred mine to his discarded tenement. Practically, that is, he has changed bodies. But how such a change may be possible is without the range of my philosophy. I have been a materialist for all my thinking life, but here, suddenly, is a clear case of man's detachability from matter.

One desperate experiment I am about to try. I sit writing here before putting the matter to issue. This morning, with the help of a table-knife that I had secreted at breakfast, I succeeded in breaking open a fairly obvious secret drawer in this wrecked writing-desk. I discovered nothing save a little green glass phial containing a white powder. Round the neck of the phial, was a label, and thereon was written this one word, " *Release*." This may be —is most probably—poison. I can understand Elvesham placing poison in my way, and I should be sure that it was his intention so to get rid of the only living witness against him, were it not for this careful concealment. The man has practically solved the problem of immortality. Save for the spite of chance, he will live in my body until it has aged, and then, again, throwing aside, he will assume some other victim's youth and strength. When one remembers his heartlessness, it is terrible to think of the ever-growing experience that . . . How long has he been leaping from body to body ? . . . But I tire of writing. The powder appears to be soluble in water. The taste is not unpleasant.

There the narrative found upon Mr. Elvesham's desk ends. His dead body lay between the desk and the chair. The latter had been pushed back, probably by his last convulsions. The story was written in pencil, and in a crazy hand, quite unlike his usual minute characters. There remain only two curious facts to record. Indisputably there was some connection between Eden and Elvesham, since the whole of Elvesham's property was bequeathed to the young man. But he never inherited. When Elvesham committed suicide, Eden was, strangely enough, already dead. Twenty-four hours before, he had been knocked down by a cab and killed instantly, at the crowded crossing at the intersection of Gower Street and Euston Road. So that the only human being who could have thrown light upon this fantastic narrative is beyond the reach of questions. Without further comment I leave this extraordinary matter to the reader's individual judgment.

THE TEMPTATION OF HARRINGAY

IT is quite impossible to say whether this thing really happened. It depends entirely on the word of R. M. Harringay, who is an artist.

Following his version of the affair, the narrative deposes that Harringay went into his studio about ten o'clock to see what he could make of the head that he had been working at the day before. The head in question was that of an Italian organ-grinder, and Harringay thought—but was not quite sure—that the title would be the "Vigil." So far he is frank, and his narrative bears the stamp of truth. He had seen the man expectant for pennies, and with a promptness that suggested genius, had had him in at once.

"Kneel. Look up at that bracket," said Harringay. "As if you expected pennies."

"Don't *grin*!" said Harringay. "I don't want to paint your gums. Look as though you were unhappy."

Now, after a night's rest, the picture proved decidedly unsatisfactory. "It's good work," said Harringay. "That little bit in the neck . . . But."

He walked about the studio and looked at the thing from this point and from that. Then he said a wicked word. In the original the word is given.

"Painting," he says he said. "Just a painting of an organ-grinder—a mere portrait. If it was a live organ-grinder I wouldn't mind. But somehow I never make things alive. I wonder if my imagination is wrong." This, too, has a truthful air. His imagination *is* wrong.

"That creative touch! To take canvas and pigment and make a man—as Adam was made—of red ochre! But this thing! If you met it walking about the streets you would know it was only a studio production. The little boys would tell it to 'Garnome and git frimed.' Some little touch . . . Well—it won't do as it is."

He went to the blinds and began to pull them down. They were made of blue holland with the rollers at the bottom of the window, so that you pull them down to get more light. He gathered his palette, brushes, and mahl-stick from his table. Then he turned to the picture and put a speck of brown in the corner of the mouth ; and shifted his attention thence to the pupil of the eye. Then he decided that the chin was a trifle too impassive for a vigil.

Presently he put down his impedimenta, and, lighting a pipe, surveyed the progress of his work. " I'm hanged if the thing isn't sneering at me," said Harringay, and he still believes it sneered.

The animation of the figure had certainly increased, but scarcely in the direction he wished. There was no mistake about the sneer. " Vigil of the Unbeliever," said Harringay. " Rather subtle and clever that ! But the left eyebrow isn't cynical enough."

He went and dabbed at the eyebrow, and added a little to the lobe of the ear to suggest materialism. Further consideration ensued. " Vigil's off, I'm afraid," said Harringay. " Why not Mephistopheles ? But that's a bit *too* common. ' A Friend of the Doge '—not so seedy. The armour won't do, though. Too Camelot. How about a scarlet robe and call him ' One of the Sacred College ' ? Humour in that, and an appreciation of Middle Italian History.

" There's always Benvenuto Cellini," said Harringay ; " with a clever suggestion of a gold cup in one corner. But that would scarcely suit the complexion."

He describes himself as babbling in this way in order to keep down an unaccountably unpleasant sensation of fear. The thing was certainly acquiring anything but a pleasing expression. Yet it was as certainly becoming far more of a living thing than it had been—if a sinister one—far more alive than anything he had ever painted before. " Call it ' Portrait of a Gentleman '," said Harringay—" ' A Certain Gentleman '.

" Won't do," said Harringay, still keeping up his courage. " Kind of thing they call Bad Taste. That sneer will have to come out. That gone, and a little more fire in the eye— never noticed how warm his eye was before—and he might do for—? What price Passionate Pilgrim? But that devilish face won't do—*this* side of the Channel.

"Some little inaccuracy does it," he said ; "eyebrows probably too oblique "—therewith pulling the blind lower to get a better light, and resuming palette and brushes.

The face on the canvas seemed animated by a spirit of its own. Where the expression of diablerie came in, he found impossible to discover—Experiment was necessary. The eyebrows—it could scarcely be the eyebrows? But he altered them. No, that was no better ; in fact, if anything, a trifle more satanic. The corner of the mouth? Pah ! more than ever a leer—and now, retouched, it was ominously grim. The eye, then? Catastrophe ! he had filled his brush with vermilion instead of brown, and yet he had felt sure it was brown ! The eye seemed now to have rolled in its socket, and was glaring at him an eye of fire. In a flash of passion, possibly with something of the courage of panic, he struck the brush full of bright red athwart the picture ; and then a very curious thing, a very strange thing indeed, occurred—if it *did* occur.

The diabolified Italian before him shut both his eyes, pursed his mouth, and wiped the colour off his face with his hand.

Then the *red eye* opened again, with a sound like the opening of lips, and the face smiled. "That was rather hasty of you," said the picture.

Harringay states that, now that the worst had happened, his self-possession returned. He had a saving persuasion that devils were reasonable creatures.

"Why do you keep moving about then," he said, "making faces and all that—sneering and squinting, while I am painting you ? "

"I don't," said the picture.

"You *do*," said Harringay.

"It's yourself," said the picture.

"It's *not* myself," said Harringay.

"It *is* yourself," said the picture. "No ! don't go hitting me with paint again, because it's true. You have been trying to fluke an expression on my face all the morning. Really, you haven't an idea what your picture ought to look like."

" I have," said Harringay.

" You have *not*," said the picture. " You *never* have with your pictures. You always start with the vaguest presentiment of what you are going to do ; it is to be something beautiful—you are sure of that—and devout, perhaps, or tragic ; but beyond that it is all experiment and chance. My dear fellow ! you don't think you can paint a picture like that ? "

Now it must be remembered that for what follows we have only Harringay's word.

" I shall paint a picture exactly as I like," said Harringay calmly.

This seemed to disconcert the picture a little. " You can't paint a picture without an inspiration," it remarked.

" But I *had* an inspiration—for this."

" Inspiration ! " sneered the sardonic figure, " a fancy that came from your seeing an organ-grinder looking up at a window ! Vigil ! Ha, ha ! You just started painting on the chance of something coming—that's what you did. And when I saw you at it I came. I want a talk with you ! "

" Art, with you," said the picture—" it's a poor business. You potter. I don't know how it is, but you don't seem able to throw your soul into it. You know too much. It hampers you. In the midst of your enthusiasms you ask yourself whether something like this has not been done before. And . . ."

" Look here," said Harringay, who had expected something better than criticism from the devil. " Are you going to talk studio with me ? " He filled his number twelve hoghair with red paint.

" The true artist," said the picture, " is always an ignorant man. An artist who theorises about his work is no longer artist but critic. Wagner . . . I say ! What's that red paint for ? "

" I'm going to paint you out," said Harringay. " I don't want to hear all that tommy-rot. If you think just because I'm an artist by trade, I'm going to talk studio to you, you make a precious mistake."

" One minute," said the picture, evidently alarmed.

122

"I want to make you an offer—a genuine offer. It's right what I'm saying. You lack inspirations. Well. No doubt you've heard of the Cathedral of Cologne, and the Devil's Bridge, and——"

"Rubbish," said Harringay. "Do you think I want to go to perdition simply for the pleasure of painting a good picture, and getting it slated. Take that."

His blood was up. His danger only nerved him to action, so he says. So he planted a dab of vermilion in his creature's mouth. The Italian spluttered and tried to wipe it off—evidently horribly surprised. And then—according to Harringay—there began a very remarkable struggle, Harringay splashing away with the red paint, and the picture wriggling about and wiping if off as fast as he put it on. "*Two* masterpieces," said the demon. "Two indubitable masterpieces for a Chelsea artist's soul. It's a bargain?" Harringay replied with the paint brush.

For a few minutes nothing could be heard but the brush going and the spluttering and ejaculations of the Italian. A lot of the strokes he caught on his arm and hand, though Harringay got over his guard often enough. Presently the paint on the palette gave out and the two antagonists stood breathless, regarding each other. The picture was so smeared with red that it looked as if it had been rolling about a slaughterhouse, and it was painfully out of breath and very uncomfortable with the wet paint trickling down its neck. Still, the first round was in its favour on the whole. "Think," it said, sticking pluckily to its point, "two supreme masterpieces—in different styles. Each equivalent to the Cathedral . . ."

"*I* know," said Harringay, and rushed out of the studio and along the passage towards his wife's boudoir.

In another minute he was back with a large tin of enamel —Hedge Sparrow's Egg Tint, it was, and a brush. At the sight of that the artistic devil with the red eye began to scream. "*Three* masterpieces—culminating masterpieces."

Harringay delivered cut two across the demon, and followed with a thrust in the eye. There was an indistinct rumbling. "*Four* masterpieces," and a spitting sound.

But Harringay had the upper hand now and meant to

keep it. With rapid, bold strokes he continued to paint over the writhing canvas, until at last it was a uniform field of shining Hedge Sparrow tint. Once the mouth reappeared and got as far as " Five master——" before he filled it with enamel ; and near the end the red eye opened and glared at him indignantly. But at last nothing remained save a gleaming panel of drying enamel. For a little while a faint stirring beneath the surface puckered it slightly here and there, but presently even that died away and the thing was perfectly still.

Then Harringay—according to Harringay's account— lit his pipe and sat down and stared at the enamelled canvas, and tried to make out clearly what had happened. Then he walked round behind it, to see if the back of it was at all remarkable. Then it was he began to regret he had not photographed the Devil before he painted him out.

This is Harringay's story—not mine. He supports it by a small canvas (24 by 20) enamelled a pale green, and by violent asseverations. It is also true that he never has produced a masterpiece, and, in the opinion of his intimate friends, probably never will.

THE STORY OF THE
INEXPERIENCED GHOST

THE SCENE amidst which Clayton told his last story comes back very vividly to my mind. There he sat, for the greater part of the time, in the corner of the authentic settle by the spacious open fire, and Sanderson sat beside him smoking the Broseley clay that bore his name. There was Evans, and that marvel among actors, Wish, who is also a modest man. We had all come down to the Mermaid Club that Saturday morning, except Clayton, who had slept there overnight—which indeed gave him the opening of his story. We had golfed until golfing was invisible ; we had dined, and we were in that mood of tranquil kindliness when men will suffer a story. When Clayton began to tell one, we naturally supposed he was lying. It may be that indeed he was lying—of that the reader will speedily be able to judge as well as I. He began, it is true, with an air of matter-of-fact anecdote, but that we thought was only the incurable artifice of the man.

" I say ! " he remarked, after a long consideration of the upward rain of sparks from the log that Sanderson had thumped, " you know I was alone here last night ? "

" Except for the domestics," said Wish.

" Who sleep in the other wing," said Clayton. " Yes. Well——" He pulled at his cigar for some little time as though he still hesitated about his confidence. Then he said, quite quietly, " I caught a ghost ! "

" Caught a ghost, did you ? " said Sanderson. " Where is it ? "

And Evans, who admires Clayton immensely and has been four weeks in America, shouted, " *Caught* a ghost, did you, Clayton ? I'm glad of it ! Tell us all about it right now."

Clayton said he would in a minute, and asked him to shut the door.

He looked apologetically at me. "There's no eaves-dropping, of course, but we don't want to upset our very excellent service with any rumours of ghosts in the place. There's too much shadow and oak panelling to trifle with that. And this, you know, wasn't a regular ghost. I don't think it will come again—ever."

"You mean to say you didn't keep it?" said Sanderson.

"I hadn't the heart to," said Clayton.

And Sanderson said he was surprised.

We laughed, and Clayton looked aggrieved. "I know," he said, with a flicker of a smile, "but the fact is it really *was* a ghost, and I'm as sure of it as I am that I am talking to you now. I'm not joking. I mean what I say."

Sanderson drew deeply at his pipe, with one reddish eye on Clayton, and then emitted a thin jet of smoke more eloquent than many words.

Clayton ignored the comment. "It is the strangest thing that has ever happened in my life. You know I never believed in ghosts or anything of the sort, before, ever; and then, you know, I bag one in a corner; and the whole business is in my hands."

He meditated still more profoundly and produced, and began to pierce, a second cigar with a curious little stabber he affected.

"You talked to it?" asked Wish.

"For the space, probably, of an hour."

"Chatty?" I said, joining the party of sceptics.

"The poor devil was in trouble," said Clayton, bowed over his cigar-end and with the very faintest note of reproof.

"Sobbing?" someone asked.

Clayton heaved a realistic sigh at the memory. "Good Lord!" he said; "yes." And then, "Poor fellow! yes."

"Where did you strike it?" asked Evans, in his best American accent.

"I never realised," said Clayton, ignoring him, "the poor sort of thing a ghost might be," and he hung us up again for a time, while he sought for matches in his pocket and lit and warmed to his cigar.

"I took an advantage," he reflected at last.

We were none of us in a hurry. " A character," he said,
" remains just the same character for all that it's been disembodied. That's a thing we too often forget. People
with a certain strength or fixity of purpose may have ghosts
of a certain strength and fixity of purpose—most haunting
ghosts, you know, must be as one-idea'd as monomaniacs
and as obstinate as mules to come back again and
again. This poor creature wasn't." He suddenly looked up
rather queerly, and his eye went round the room. " I
say it," he said, " in all kindliness, but that is the plain
truth of the case. Even at the first glance he struck me as
weak."

He punctuated with the help of his cigar.

" I came upon him, you know, in the long passage. His
back was towards me and I saw him first. Right off I knew
him for a ghost. He was transparent and whitish ; clean
through his chest I could see the glimmer of the little
window at the end. And not only his physique but his
attitude struck me as being weak. He looked, you know,
as though he didn't know in the slightest whatever he
meant to do. One hand was on the panelling and the
other fluttered to his mouth. Like—*so* ! "

" What sort of physique ? " said Sanderson.

" Lean. You know that sort of young man's neck that
has two great flutings down the back, here and here—so !
And a little, meanish head with scrubby hair and rather
bad ears. Shoulders bad, narrower than the hips ; turn-
down collar, ready-made short jacket, trousers baggy and
a little frayed at the heels. That's how he took me. I
came very quietly up the staircase. I did not carry a light,
you know—the candles are on the landing table and there
is that lamp—and I was in my list slippers, and I saw him
as I came up. I stopped dead at that—taking him in. I
wasn't a bit afraid. I think that in most of these affairs one
is never nearly so afraid or excited as one imagines one
would be. I was surprised and interested. I thought,
' Good Lord ! Here's a ghost at last ! And I haven't
believed for a moment in ghosts during the last five-and-
twenty years.' "

" Um," said Wish.

127

" I suppose I wasn't on the landing a moment before he found out I was there. He turned on me sharply, and I saw the face of an immature young man, a weak nose, a scrubby little moustache, a feeble chin. So for an instant we stood—he looking over his shoulder at me—and regarded one another. Then he seemed to remember his high calling. He turned round, drew himself up, projected his face, raised his arms, spread his hands in approved ghost fashion—came towards me. As he did so his little jaw dropped, and he emitted a faint, drawn-out ' Boo.' No, it wasn't—not a bit dreadful. I'd dined. I'd had a bottle of champagne, and being all alone, perhaps two or three—perhaps even four or five—whiskies, so I was as solid as rocks and no more frightened than if I'd been assailed by a frog. ' Boo ! ' I said. ' Nonsense. You don't belong to *this* place. What are you doing here ? '

" I could see him wince. ' Boo-oo,' he said.

" ' Boo—be hanged ! Are you a member ? ' I said ; and just to show I didn't care a pin for him I stepped through a corner of him and made to light my candle. ' Are you a member ? ' I repeated, looking at him sideways.

" He moved a little so as to stand clear of me, and his bearing became crestfallen. ' No,' he said, in answer to the persistent interrogation of my eye ; ' I'm not a member —I'm a ghost.'

" ' Well, that doesn't give you the run of the Mermaid Club. Is there anyone you want to see, or anything of that sort ? ' And doing it as steadily as possible for fear that he should mistake the carelessness of whisky for the distraction of fear, I got my candle alight. I turned on him, holding it. ' What are you doing here ? ' I said.

" He had dropped his hands and stopped his booing, and there he stood, abashed and awkward, the ghost of a weak, silly, aimless young man. ' I'm haunting,' he said.

" ' You haven't any business to,' I said, in a quiet voice.

" ' I'm a ghost,' he said, as if in defence.

" ' That may be, but you haven't any business to haunt here. This is a respectable private club ; people often stop here with nursemaids and children, and, going about in the careless way you do, some poor little mite could

128

easily come upon you and be scared out of her wits. I suppose you didn't think of that?'

"'No sir,' he said, 'I didn't.'

"'You should have done. You haven't any claim on the place, have you? Weren't murdered here, or anything of that sort?'

"'None, sir; but I thought as it was old and oak-panelled——'

"'That's *no* excuse.' I regarded him firmly. 'Your coming here is a mistake,' I said, in a tone of friendly superiority. I feigned to see if I had my matches, and then looked up at him frankly. 'If I were you, I wouldn't wait for cock-crow—I'd vanish right away.'

"He looked embarrassed. 'The fact *is*, sir——' he began.

"'I'd vanish,' I said, driving it home.

"'The fact is, sir, that—somehow—I can't.'

"'You *can't*?'

"'No, sir. There's something I've forgotten. I've been hanging about here since midnight last night, hiding in the cupboards of the empty bedrooms and things like that. I'm flurried. I've never come haunting before, and it seems to put me out.'

"'Put you out?'

"'Yes, sir. I've tried to do it several times, and it doesn't come off. There's some little thing has slipped me, and I can't get back.'

"That, you know, rather bowled me over. He looked at me in such an abject way that for the life of me I couldn't keep up quite the high, hectoring vein I had adopted. 'That's queer,' I said, and, as I spoke, I fancied I heard someone moving about down below. 'Come into my room and tell me more about it,' I said. I didn't, of course, understand this, and I tried to take him by the arm. But, of course, you might as well have tried to take hold of a puff of smoke! I had forgotten my number, I think; anyhow, I remember going into several bedrooms—it was lucky I was the only soul in that wing—until I saw my traps. 'Here we are,' I said, and sat down in the arm-chair; 'sit down and tell me all about it. It seems to me you have got yourself into a jolly awkward position, old chap.'

" Well, he said he wouldn't sit down ; he'd prefer to flit up and down the room if it was all the same to me. And so he did, and in a little while we were deep in a long and serious talk. And presently, you know, something of those whiskies and sodas evaporated out of me, and I began to realise just a little what a thundering rum and weird business it was that I was in. There he was, semi-transparent—the proper conventional phantom, and noiseless except for his ghost of a voice—flitting to and fro in that nice, clean, chintz-hung old bedroom. You could see the gleam of the copper candlesticks through him, and the lights on the brass fender, and the corners of the framed engravings on the wall, and there he was telling me all about this wretched little life of his that had recently ended on earth. He hadn't a particularly honest face, you know, but being transparent, of course, he couldn't avoid telling the truth."

" Eh ? " said Wish, suddenly sitting up in his chair.

" What ? " said Clayton.

" Being transparent—couldn't avoid telling the truth—I don't see it," said Wish.

" *I* don't see it," said Clayton, with inimitable assurance. " But it *is* so, I can assure you, nevertheless. I don't believe he got once a nail's breadth off the Bible truth. He told me how he had been killed—he went down into a London basement with a candle to look for a leakage of gas—and described himself as a senior English master in a London private school when that release occurred."

" Poor wretch ! " said I.

" That's what I thought, and the more he talked the more I thought it. There he was, purposeless in life and purposeless out of it. He talked of his father and mother and his schoolmaster, and all who had ever been anything to him in the world, meanly. He had been too sensitive, too nervous ; none of them had ever valued him properly or understood him, he said. He had never had a real friend in the world, I think ; he had never had a success. He had shirked games and failed examinations. ' It's like that with some people,' he said ; ' whenever I got into the examination-room or anywhere, everything seemed to go.' Engaged to be married, of course—to another over-sensitive person, I suppose—when the indiscretion with the gas escape ended his affairs. ' And where are you now ? ' I asked. ' Not in——? '

" He wasn't clear on that point at all. The impression he gave me was of a sort of vague, intermediate state, a special reserve for souls too non-existent for anything so positive as either sin or virtue. *I* don't know. He was much too egotistical and unobservant to give me any clear idea of the kind of place, kind of country, there is on the Other Side of Things. Wherever he was he seems to have fallen in with a set of kindred spirits : ghosts of weak Cockney young men, who were on a footing of Christian names, and among these there was certainly a lot of talk about ' going haunting ' and things like that. Yes—going haunting ! They seemed to think ' haunting ' a tremendous adventure, and most of them funked it all the time. And so primed, you know, he had come."

" But really ! " said Wish to the fire.

" These are the impressions he gave me, anyhow," said Clayton modestly. " I may, of course, have been in a rather uncritical state, but that was the sort of background he gave to himself. He kept flitting up and down, with his thin voice going—talking, talking about his wretched self, and never a word of clear, firm statement from first to last. He was thinner and sillier and more pointless than if he had been real and alive. Only then, you know, he would not have been in my bedroom here—if he *had* been alive. I should have kicked him out."

" Of course," said Evans, " there *are* poor mortals like that."

" And there's just as much chance of their having ghosts as the rest of us," I admitted.

" What gave a sort of point to him, you know, was the fact that he did seem within limits to have found himself out. The mess he had made of haunting had depressed him terribly. He had been told it would be a ' lark ' ; he had come expecting it to be a ' lark,' and here it was, nothing but another failure added to his record ! He proclaimed himself an utter out-and-out failure. He said, and I can quite believe it, that he had never tried to do anything all his life that he hadn't made a perfect mess of—and through all the wastes of eternity he never would. If he had had sympathy, perhaps—— He paused at that, and stood regarding me. He remarked that, strange as it might seem to me, nobody, not any one, ever, had given him the amount of sympathy I was doing now. I could see what he wanted straight away, and I determined to head him off at once. I may be a brute, you know, but being the Only Real Friend, the recipient of the confidences of one of these egotistical weaklings, ghost or body, is beyond my physical endurance. I got up briskly. 'Don't you brood on these things too much,' I said. 'The thing you've got to do is to get out of this—get out of this sharp. You pull yourself together and *try*.' 'I can't,' he said. 'You try,' I said, and try he did.''

"Try !" said Sanderson. "*How* ?"

"Passes," said Clayton.

"Passes ?"

"Complicated series of gestures and passes with the hands. That's how he had come in and that's how he had to get out again. Lord ! what a business I had !"

"But how could *any* series of passes——" I began.

"My dear man," said Clayton, turning on me and putting a great emphasis on certain words, "you want *everything* clear. *I* don't know *how*. All I know is that you *do*—that *he* did, anyhow, at least. After a fearful time, you know, he got his passes right and suddenly disappeared."

"Did you," said Sanderson, slowly, "observe the passes ?"

"Yes," said Clayton, and seemed to think, "It was tremendously queer," he said. "There we were, I and this thin vague ghost, in that silent room, in this silent, empty inn, in this silent little Friday-night town. Not a sound except our voices and a faint panting he made when he swung. There was the bedroom candle, and one candle on the dressing-table alight, that was all—sometimes one

132

or other would flare up into a tall, lean, astonished flame for a space. And queer things happened. ' I can't,' he said ; ' I shall never——! ' And suddenly he sat down on a little chair at the foot of the bed and began to sob and sob. Lord ! what a harrowing, whimpering thing he seemed !

" ' You pull yourself together,' I said, and tried to pat him on the back, and . . . my confounded hand went through him ! By that time, you know, I wasn't nearly so—massive as I had been on the landing. I got the queerness of it full. I remember snatching back my hand out of him, as it were, with a little thrill, and walking over to the dressing-table. ' You pull yourself together,' I said to him, ' and try.' And in order to encourage and help him, I began to try as well."

" What ! " said Sanderson, " the passes ? "

" Yes, the passes."

" But——" I said, moved by an idea that eluded me for a space.

" This is interesting," said Sanderson, with his finger in his pipe-bowl. " You mean to say this ghost of yours gave away——"

" Did his level best to give away the whole confounded barrier ? *Yes.*"

" He didn't," said Wish ; " he couldn't. Or you'd have gone there too."

" That's precisely it," I said, finding my elusive idea put into words for me.

" That *is* precisely it," said Clayton, with thoughtful eyes upon the fire.

For just a little while there was silence.

" And at last he did it ? " said Sanderson.

" At last he did it. I had to keep him up to it hard, but he did it at last—rather suddenly. He despaired, we had a scene, and then he got up abruptly and asked me to go through the whole performance, slowly, so that he might see. ' I believe,' he said, ' if I could *see* I should spot what was wrong at once.' And he did. ' *I* know,' he said. ' What do you know ? ' said I. ' *I* know,' he repeated. Then he said peevishly, ' I *can't* do it if you look at me—

133

I really *can't* ; it's been that, partly, all along. I'm such a nervous fellow that you put me out.' Well, we had a bit of an argument. Naturally I wanted to see ; but he was as obstinate as a mule, and suddenly I had come over as tired as a dog—he tired me out. 'All right,' I said, '*I* won't look at you,' and turned towards the mirror, on the wardrobe, by the bed.

"He started off very fast. I tried to follow him by looking in the looking-glass, to see just what it was had hung. Round went his arms and hands, so, and so, and so, and then with a rush came to the last gesture of all—you stand erect and open out your arms—and so, don't you know, he stood. And then he didn't ! He didn't ! He wasn't ! I wheeled round from the looking-glass to him. There was nothing ! I was alone with the flaring candles and a staggering mind. What had happened ? Had anything happened ? Had I been dreaming ? . . . And then, with an absurd note of finality about it, the clock upon the landing discovered the moment was ripe for striking *one*. So !— Ping ! And I was as grave and sober as a judge, with all my champagne and whisky gone into the vast serene. Feeling queer, you know—confoundedly *queer* ! Queer ! Good Lord ! "

He regarded his cigar-ash for a moment. "That's all that happened," he said.

" And then you went to bed ? " asked Evans.

" What else was there to do ? "

I looked Wish in the eye. We wanted to scoff, and there was something, something perhaps in Clayton's voice and manner, that hampered our desire.

" And about these passes ? " said Sanderson.

" I believe I could do them now."

" Oh ! " said Sanderson, and produced a pen-knife and set himself to grub the dottle out of the bowl of his clay.

" Why don't you do them now ? " said Sanderson, shutting his pen-knife with a click.

" That's what I'm going to do," said Clayton.

" They won't work," said Evans.

" If they do——" I suggested.

" You know, I'd rather you didn't," said Wish, stretching out his legs.

" Why ? " asked Evans.

" I'd rather he didn't," said Wish.

" But he hasn't got 'em right," said Sanderson, plugging too much tobacco into his pipe.

" All the same, I'd rather he didn't," said Wish.

We argued with Wish. He said that for Clayton to go through those gestures was like mocking a serious matter. " But you don't believe——? " I said. Wish glanced at Clayton, who was staring into the fire, weighing something in his mind. " I do—more than half, anyhow, I do," said Wish.

" Clayton," said I, " you're too good a liar for us. Most of it was all right. But that disappearance . . . happened to be convincing. Tell us, it's a tale of cock and bull."

He stood up without heeding me, took the middle of the hearthrug, and faced me. For a moment he regarded his feet thoughtfully, and then for all the rest of the time his eyes were on the opposite wall, with an intent expression. He raised his two hands slowly to the level of his eyes and so began. . . .

Now, Sanderson is a Freemason, a member of the lodge of the Four Kings, which devotes itself so ably to the study and elucidation of all the mysteries of Masonry past and present, and among the students of this lodge Sanderson is by no means the least. He followed Clayton's motions with a singular interest in his reddish eye. " That's not bad," he said, when it was done. " You really do, you know, put things together, Clayton, in a most amazing fashion. But there's one little detail out."

" I know," said Clayton. " I believe I could tell you which."

" Well ? "

" This," said Clayton, and did a queer little twist and writhing and thrust of the hands.

" Yes."

" That, you know, was what *he* couldn't get right," said Clayton. " But how do *you*——? "

" Most of this business, and particularly how you

invented it, I don't understand at all," said Sanderson, "but just that phase—I do." He reflected. "These happen to be a series of gestures—connected with a certain branch of esoteric Masonry—— Probably you know. Or else—— *How*?" He reflected still further. "I do not see I can do any harm in telling you just the proper twist. After all, if you know, you know; if you don't, you don't."

"I know nothing," said Clayton, "except what the poor devil let out last night."

"Well, anyhow," said Sanderson, and placed his church-warden very carefully upon the shelf over the fireplace Then very rapidly he gesticulated with his hands.

"So?" said Clayton, repeating.

"So," said Sanderson, and took his pipe in hand again.

"Ah, *now*," said Clayton, "I can do the whole thing—right."

He stood up before the waning fire and smiled at us all. But I think there was just a little hesitation in his smile. "If I begin——" he said.

"I wouldn't begin," said Wish.

"It's all right!" said Evans. "Matter is indestructible. You don't think any jiggery-pokery of this sort is going to snatch Clayton into the world of shades. Not it! You may try, Clayton, so far as I'm concerned, until your arms drop off at the wrists."

"I don't believe that," said Wish, and stood up and put his arm on Clayton's shoulder. "You've made me half believe in that story somehow, and I don't want to see the thing done."

"Goodness!" said I, "here's Wish frightened!"

"I am," said Wish, with real or admirably feigned intensity. "I believe that if he goes through these motions right, he'll *go*."

"He'll not do anything of the sort," I cried. "There's only one way out of this world for men, and Clayton is thirty years from that. Besides . . . And such a ghost! Do you think——?"

Wish interrupted me by moving. He walked out from

among our chairs and stopped beside the table and stood there. " Clayton," he said, " you're a fool."

Clayton, with a humorous light in his eyes, smiled back at him. " Wish," he said, " is right and all you others are wrong. I shall go. I shall get to the end of these passes, and as the last swish whistles through the air, Presto !— this hearthrug will be vacant, the room will be blank amazement, and a respectably dressed gentleman of fifteen stone will plump into the world of shades. I'm certain. So will you be. I decline to argue further. Let the thing be tried."

" *No*," said Wish, and made a step and ceased, and Clayton raised his hands once more to repeat the spirit's passing.

By that time, you know, we were all in a state of tension —largely because of the behaviour of Wish. We sat all of us with our eyes on Clayton—I, at least, with a sort of tight, stiff feeling about me as though from the back of my skull to the middle of my thighs my body had been changed to steel. And there, with a gravity that was imperturbably serene, Clayton bowed and swayed and waved his hands and arms before us. As he drew towards the end one piled up, one tingled in one's teeth. The last gesture, I have said, was to swing the arms out wide open, with the face held up. And when at last he swung out to this closing gesture, I ceased even to breathe. It was ridiculous, of course, but you know that ghost-story feeling. It was after dinner, in a queer, old shadowy house. Would he, after all——?

There he stood for one stupendous moment, with his arms open and his upturned face, assured and bright, in the glare of the hanging lamp. We hung through that moment as if it were an age, and then came from all of us something that was half a sigh of infinite relief and half a reassuring " *No* ! " For visibly—he wasn't going. It was all nonsense. He had told an idle story, and carried it almost to conviction, that was all ! . . . And then in that moment the face of Clayton changed.

It changed. It changed as a lit house changes when its lights are suddenly extinguished. His eyes were suddenly eyes that were fixed, his smile was frozen on his lips, and he stood there still. He stood there, very gently swaying.

That moment, too, was an age. And then, you know, chairs were scraping, things were falling, and we were all moving. His knees seemed to give, and he fell forward, and Evans rose and caught him in his arms. . . .

It stunned us all. For a minute, I suppose, no one said a coherent thing. We believed it, yet could not believe it. . . . I came out of a muddled stupefaction to find myself kneeling beside him, and his vest and shirt were torn open, and Sanderson's hand lay on his heart. . . .

Well—the simple fact before us could very well wait our convenience ; there was no hurry for us to comprehend. It lay there for an hour ; it lies athwart my memory, black and amazing still, to this day. Clayton had, indeed, passed into the world that lies so near to and so far from our own, and he had gone thither by the only road that mortal man may take. But whether he did indeed pass there by the poor ghost's incantation, or whether he was stricken suddenly by apoplexy in the midst of an idle tale—as the coroner's jury would have us believe—is no matter for my judging ; it is just one of those inexplicable riddles that must remain unsolved until the final solution of all things shall come. All I certainly know is that, in the very moment, in the very instant, of concluding those passes, he changed, and staggered, and fell down before us—dead !

THE STOLEN BODY

M<small>R.</small> B<small>ESSEL</small> was the senior partner in the firm of Bessel, Hart, and Brown, of St. Paul's Churchyard, and for many years he was well known among those interested in psychical research as a liberal-minded and conscientious investigator. He was an unmarried man, and instead of living in the suburbs, after the fashion of his class, he occupied rooms in the Albany, near Piccadilly. He was particularly interested in the questions of thought transference and of apparitions of the living, and in November, 1896, he commenced a series of experiments in conjunction with Mr. Vincey, of Staple Inn, in order to test the alleged possibility of projecting an apparition of oneself by force of will through space.

Their experiments were conducted in the following manner : At a pre-arranged hour Mr. Bessel shut himself in one of his rooms in the Albany and Mr. Vincey in his sitting-room in the Staple Inn, and each then fixed his mind as resolutely as possible on the other. Mr. Bessel had acquired the art of self-hypnotism, and, so far as he could, he attempted first to hypnotise himself and then to project himself as a " phantom of the living " across the intervening space of nearly two miles into Mr. Vincey's apartment. On several evenings this was tried without any satisfactory result, but on the fifth or sixth occasion Mr. Vincey did actually see or imagine he saw an apparition of Mr. Bessel standing in his room. He states that the appearance, although brief, was very vivid and real. He noticed that Mr. Bessel's face was white and his expression anxious, and, moreover, that his hair was disordered. For a moment Mr. Vincey, in spite of his state of expectation, was too surprised to speak or move, and in that moment it seemed to him as though the figure glanced over its shoulder and incontinently vanished.

It had been arranged that an attempt should be made to photograph any phantasm seen, but Mr. Vincey had not the instant presence of mind to snap the camera that lay ready on the table beside him, and when he did so he was too late. Greatly elated, however, even by this partial success, he made a note of the exact time, and at once took a cab to the Albany to inform Mr. Bessel of this result.

He was surprised to find Mr. Bessel's outer door standing open to the night, and the inner apartments lit and in an extraordinary disorder. An empty champagne magnum lay smashed upon the floor ; its neck had been broken off against the inkpot on the bureau and lay beside it. An octagonal occasional table, which carried a bronze statuette and a number of choice books, had been rudely overturned, and down the primrose paper of the wall inky fingers had been drawn, as it seemed for the mere pleasure of defilement. One of the delicate chintz curtains had been violently torn from its rings and thrust upon the fire, so that the smell of its smouldering filled the room. Indeed the whole place was disarranged in the strangest fashion. For a few minutes Mr. Vincey, who had entered sure of finding Mr. Bessel in his easy chair awaiting him, could scarcely believe his eyes, and stood staring helplessly at these unanticipated things.

Then, full of a vague sense of calamity, he sought the porter at the entrance lodge. " Where is Mr. Bessel ? " he asked. " Do you know that all the furniture is broken in Mr. Bessel's room ? " The porter said nothing, but, obeying his gestures, came at once to Mr. Bessel's apartment to see the state of affairs. " This settles it," he said, surveying the lunatic confusion. " I didn't know of this. Mr. Bessel's gone off. He's mad ! "

He then proceeded to tell Mr. Vincey that about half an hour previously, that is to say, at about the time of Mr. Bessel's apparition in Mr. Vincey's rooms, the missing gentleman had rushed out of the gates of the Albany into Vigo Street, hatless and with disordered hair, and had vanished into the direction of Bond Street. " And as he went past me," said the porter, " he laughed—a sort of gasping laugh, with his mouth open and his eyes glaring— I tell you, sir, he fair scared me !—like this."

According to his imitation it was anything but a pleasant

laugh. "He waved his hand, with all his fingers crooked and clawing—like that. And he said, in a sort of fierce whisper, ' *Life* ! ' Just that one word, ' *Life* ! ' "

"Dear me," said Mr. Vincey. "Tut, tut," and "Dear me ! " He could think of nothing else to say. He was naturally very much surprised. He turned from the room to the porter and from the porter to the room in the gravest perplexity. Beyond his suggestion that probably Mr. Bessel would come back presently and explain what had happened, their conversation was unable to proceed. " It might be a sudden toothache," said the porter, " a very sudden and violent toothache, jumping on him suddenly-like and driving him wild. I've broken things myself before now in such a case . . ." He thought. " If it was, why should he say ' *life* ' to me as he went past ? "

Mr. Vincey did not know. Mr. Bessel did not return, and at last Mr. Vincey, having done some more helpless staring, and having addressed a note of brief inquiry and left it in a conspicuous position on the bureau, returned in a very perplexed frame of mind to his own premises in Staple Inn. This affair had given him a shock. He was at a loss to account for Mr. Bessel's conduct on any sane hypothesis. He tried to read, but he could not do so ; he went for a short walk, and was so preoccupied that he narrowly escaped a cab at the top of Chancery Lane ; and at last—a full hour before his usual time—he went to bed. For a considerable time he could not sleep because of his menory of the silent confusion of Mr. Bessel's apartment, and when at length he did attain an uneasy slumber it was at once disturbed by a very vivid and distressing dream of Mr. Bessel.

He saw Mr. Bessel gesticulating wildly, and with his face white and contorted. And, inexplicably mingled with his appearance, suggested perhaps by his gestures, was an intense fear, an urgency to act. He even believes that he heard the voice of his fellow experimenter calling distress-fully to him, though at the time he considered this to be an illusion. The vivid impression remained though Mr. Vincey awoke. For a space he lay awake and trembling in the darkness, possessed with that vague, unaccountable terror of unknown possibilities that comes out of dreams upon even the bravest men. But at last he roused himself, and turned over and went to sleep again, only for the dream to return with enhanced vividness.

He awoke with such a strong conviction that Mr. Bessel was in overwhelming distress and need of help that sleep was no longer possible. He was persuaded that his friend had rushed out to some dire calamity. For a time he lay reasoning vainly against this belief, but at last he gave way to it. He arose, against all reason, lit his gas and dressed, and set out through the deserted streets—deserted, save for a noiseless policeman or so and the early news carts—towards Vigo Street to inquire if Mr. Bessel had returned.

But he never got there. As he was going down Long Acre, some unaccountable impulse turned him aside out of that street towards Covent Garden, which was just waking to its nocturnal activities. He saw the market in front of him—a queer effect of glowing yellow lights and busy black figures. He became aware of a shouting, and perceived a figure turn the corner by the hotel and run swiftly towards him. He knew at once that it was Mr. Bessel. But it was Mr. Bessel transfigured. He was hatless and dishevelled, his collar was torn open, he grasped a bone-handled walking-cane near the ferrule end, and his mouth was pulled awry. And he ran, with agile strides, very rapidly. Their encounter was the affair of an instant. "Bessel!" cried Vincey.

The running man gave no sign of recognition, either of Mr. Vincey or of his own name. Instead, he cut at his friend savagely with the stick, hitting him in the face within an inch of the eye. Mr. Vincey, stunned and astonished, staggered back, lost his footing, and fell heavily on the pavement. It seemed to him that Mr. Bessel leapt over him as he fell. When he looked again Mr. Bessel had vanished, and a policeman and a number of garden porters and salesmen were rushing past towards Long Acre in hot pursuit.

With the assistance of several passers-by—for the whole street was speedily alive with running people—Mr. Vincey struggled to his feet. He at once became the centre of a crowd greedy to see his injury. A multitude of voices competed to reassure him of his safety, and then to tell him of the behaviour of the madman, as they regarded Mr. Bessel. He had suddenly appeared in the middle of the market, screaming "*Life! Life!*" striking right and left with a blood-stained walking-stick, and dancing and shouting with laughter at each successful blow. A lad and two women had broken heads, and he had smashed a man's wrist ; a little child had been knocked insensible, and for a time he had driven everyone before him, so furious and resolute had his behaviour been. Then he made a raid upon a coffee stall, hurled its paraffin flare through the window of the post office, and fled laughing, after stunning the foremost of the two policemen who had the pluck to charge him.

Mr. Vincey's first impulse was naturally to join in the pursuit of his friend, in order if possible to save him from the violence of the indignant people. But his action was slow, the blow had half stunned him, and while this was still no more than a resolution came the news, shouted through the crowd, that Mr. Bessel had eluded his pursuers. At first Mr. Vincey could scarcely credit this, but the universality of the report, and presently the dignified return of two futile policemen, convinced him. After some aimless inquiries he returned towards Staple Inn, padding a handkerchief to a now very painful nose.

He was angry and astonished and perplexed. It appeared to him indisputable that Mr. Bessel must have gone violently mad in the midst of his experiment in thought transference, but why that should make him appear with a sad white face in Mr. Vincey's dreams seemed a problem beyond solution. He racked his brains in vain to explain this. It seemed to him at last that not simply Mr. Bessel, but the order of things must be insane. But he could think of nothing to do. He shut himself carefully into his room, lit his fire—it was a gas fire with asbestos bricks—and, fearing fresh dreams if he went to bed, remained bathing his injured face, or holding up books in a vain attempt to read until dawn. Throughout that vigil he had a curious persuasion that Mr. Bessel was endeavouring to speak to him, but he would not let himself attend to any such belief.

About dawn, his physical fatigue asserted itself, and he

went to bed and slept at last in spite of dreaming. He rose late, unrested and anxious and in considerable facial pain. The morning papers had no news of Mr. Bessel's aberration —it had come too late for them. Mr. Vincey's perplexities, to which the fever of his bruise added fresh irritation, became at last intolerable, and, after a fruitless visit to the Albany, he went down to St. Paul's Churchyard to Mr. Hart, Mr. Bessel's partner, and so far as Mr. Vincey knew, his nearest friend.

He was surprised to learn that Mr. Hart, although he knew nothing of the outbreak, had also been disturbed by a vision, the very vision that Mr. Vincey had seen—Mr. Bessel, white and dishevelled, pleading earnestly by his gestures for help. That was his impression of the import of his signs. "I was just going to look him up in the Albany when you arrived," said Mr. Hart. "I was so sure of something being wrong with him."

As the outcome of their consultation the two gentlemen decided to inquire at Scotland Yard for news of their missing friend. "He is bound to be laid by the heels," said Mr. Hart. "He can't go on at that pace for long." But the police authorities had not laid Mr. Bessel by the heels. They confirmed Mr. Vincey's overnight experiences and added fresh circumstances, some of an even graver character than those he knew—a list of smashed glass along the upper half of Tottenham Court Road, an attack upon a policeman in Hampstead Road, and an atrocious assault upon a woman. All these outrages were committed between half-past twelve and a quarter to two in the morning, and between those hours—and, indeed, from the very moment of Mr. Bessel's first rush from his rooms at half-past nine in the evening— they could trace the deepening violence of his fantastic career. For the last hour, at least from before one, that is, until a quarter to two, he had run amuck through London, eluding with amazing agility every effort to stop or capture him.

But after a quarter to two he had vanished. Up to that hour witnesses were multitudinous. Dozens of people had seen him, fled from him or pursued him, and then things suddenly came to an end. At a quarter to two he had been seen running down the Euston Road towards Baker Street, flourishing a can of burning colza oil and jerking splashes of flame therefrom at the windows of the houses he passed. But none of the policemen on Euston Road beyond the Waxwork Exhibition, nor any of those in the side streets down which he must have passed had he left the Euston Road, had seen anything of him. Abruptly he disappeared. Nothing of his subsequent doings came to light, in spite of the keenest inquiry.

Here was a fresh astonishment for Mr. Vincey. He had found considerable comfort in Mr. Hart's conviction, " He is bound to be laid by the heels before long," and in that assurance he had been able to suspend his mental perplexities. But any fresh development seemed destined to add new possibilities to a pile already heaped beyond the powers of his acceptance. He found himself doubting whether his memory might not have played him some grotesque trick, debating whether any of these things could possibly have happened ; and in the afternoon he hunted up Mr. Hart again to share the intolerable weight on his mind. He found Mr. Hart engaged with a well-known private detective, but as that gentleman accomplished nothing in this case, we need not enlarge upon his proceedings.

All that day Mr. Bessel's whereabouts eluded an unceasingly active inquiry, and all that night. And all that day there was a persuasion in the back of Mr. Vincey's mind that Mr. Bessel sought his attention, and all through the night Mr. Bessel with a tear-stained face of anguish pursued him through his dreams. And whenever he saw Mr. Bessel in his dreams, he also saw a number of other faces, vague but malignant, that seemed to be pursuing Mr. Bessel.

It was on the following day, Sunday, that Mr. Vincey recalled certain remarkable stories of Mrs. Bullock, the medium, who was then attracting attention for the first time in London. He determined to consult her. She was staying at the house of that well-known inquirer, Dr. Wilson Paget, and Mr. Vincey, although he had never met that gentleman before, repaired to him forthwith with the intention of invoking her help. But scarcely had he mentioned the name of Bessel when Doctor Paget interrupted him.

" Last night—just at the end," he said, " we had a communication."

He left the room, and returned with a slate on which were certain words written in a handwriting, shaky indeed, but indisputably the handwriting of Mr. Bessel !

" How did you get this ? " said Mr. Vincey. " Do you mean——? "

" We got it last night," said Doctor Paget. With numerous interruptions from Mr. Vincey, he proceeded to explain how the writing had been obtained. It appears that in her *séances*, Mrs. Bullock passes into a condition of trance, her eyes rolling up in a strange way under her eyelids, and her body becoming rigid. She then begins to talk very rapidly, usually in voices other than her own. At the same time one or both of her hands may become active, and if slates and pencils are provided they will then write messages simultaneously with and quite independently of the flow of words from her mouth. By many she is considered an even more remarkable medium than the celebrated Mrs. Piper. It was one of these messages, the one written by her left hand, that Mr. Vincey now had before him. It consisted of eight words written disconnectedly " George Bessel . . . trial excav^n. . . Baker Street . . . help . . . starvation." Curiously enough, neither Doctor Paget nor the two other inquirers who were present had heard of the disappearance of Mr. Bessel—the news of it appeared only in the evening papers of Saturday—and they had put the message aside with many others of a vague and enigmatical sort that Mrs. Bullock has from time to time delivered.

When Doctor Paget heard Mr. Vincey's story, he gave himself at once with great energy to the pursuit of this clue to the discovery of Mr. Bessel. It would serve no useful purpose here to describe the inquiries of Mr. Vincey and himself ; suffice it that the clue was a genuine one, and that Mr. Bessel was actually discovered by its aid.

He was found at the bottom of a detached shaft which had been sunk and abandoned at the commencement of the work for the new electric railway near Baker Street Station. His arm and leg and two ribs were broken. The shaft is protected by a hoarding nearly 20 ft. high, and over this, incredible as it seems, Mr. Bessel, a stout, middle-aged gentleman, must have scrambled in order to fall down the shaft. He was saturated in colza oil, and the smashed tin lay beside him, but luckily the flame had been extinguished by his fall. And his madness had passed from him altogether. But he was, of course, terribly enfeebled, and at the sight of his rescuers he gave way to hysterical weeping.

In view of the deplorable state of his flat, he was taken to the house of Dr. Hatton in Upper Baker Street. Here he was subjected to a sedative treatment, and anything that might recall the violent crisis through which he had passed was carefully avoided. But on the second day he volunteered a statement.

Since that occasion Mr. Bessel has several times repeated this statement—to myself among other people—varying the details as the narrator of real experiences always does, but never by any chance contradicting himself in any particular. And the statement he makes is in substance as follows.

In order to understand it clearly it is necessary to go back to his experiments with Mr. Vincey before his remarkable attack. Mr. Bessel's first attempts at self-projection, in his experiments with Mr. Vincey, were, as the reader will remember, unsuccessful. But through all of them he was concentrating all his power and will upon getting out of the body—" willing it with all my might," he says. At last, almost against expectation, came success. And Mr. Bessel asserts that he, being alive, did actually, by an effort of will, leave his body and pass into some place or state outside this world.

The release was, he asserts, instantaneous. "At one moment I was seated in my chair, with my eyes tightly shut, my hands gripping the arms of the chair, doing all I could to concentrate my mind on Vincey, and then I perceived myself outside my body—saw my body near me, but certainly not containing me, with the hands relaxing and the head drooping forward on the breast."

Nothing shakes him in his assurance of that release. He describes in a quiet, matter-of-fact way the new sensation he experienced. He felt he had become impalpable—so much he had expected, but he had not expected to find himself enormously large. So, however, it would seem he became. " I was a great cloud—if I may express it that way—anchored to my body. It appeared to me, at first, as if I had discovered a greater self of which the conscious being in my brain was only a little part. I saw the Albany and Piccadilly and Regent Street and all the rooms and places in the houses, very minute and very bright and distinct, spread out below me like a little city seen from a balloon. Every now and then vague shapes like drifting wreaths of smoke made the vision a little indistinct, but at first I paid little heed to them. The thing that astonished me most, and which astonishes me still, is that I saw quite distinctly the insides of the houses as well as the streets, saw little people dining and talking in the private houses, men and women dining, playing billiards, and drinking in restaurants and hotels, and several places of entertainment crammed with people. It was like watching the affairs of a glass hive."

Such were Mr. Bessel's exact words as I took them down when he told me the story. Quite forgetful of Mr. Vincey, he remained for a space observing these things. Impelled by curiosity, he says, he stooped down and with the shadowy arm he found himself possessed of attempted to touch a man walking along Vigo Street. But he could not do so, though his finger seemed to pass through the man. Something prevented his doing this, but what it was he finds it hard to describe. He compares the obstacle to a sheet of glass.

" I felt as a kitten may feel," he said, " when it goes for the first time to pat its reflection in a mirror." Again and again, on the occasion when I heard him tell this story, Mr. Bessel returned to that comparison of the sheet of glass. Yet it was not altogether a precise comparison, because, as the reader will speedily see, there were interruptions of this generally impermeable resistance, means of getting through the barrier to the material world again. But, naturally, there is a very great difficulty in expressing these unprecedented impressions in the language of everyday experience.

A thing that impressed him instantly, and which weighed

upon him throughout all this experience, was the stillness of this place—he was in a world without sound.

At first Mr. Bessel's mental state was an unemotional wonder. His thought chiefly concerned itself with where he might be. He was out of the body—out of his material body, at any rate—but that was not all. He believes, and I for one believe also, that he was somewhere out of space, as we understand it, altogether. By a strenuous effort of will he had passed out of his body into a world beyond this world, a world undreamt of, yet lying so close to it and so strangely situated with regard to it that all things on this earth are clearly visible both from without and from within in this other world about us. For a long time, as it seemed to him, this realisation occupied his mind to the exclusion of all other matters, and then he recalled the engagement with Mr. Vincey, to which this astonishing experience was, after all, but a prelude.

He turned his mind to locomotion in this new body in which he found himself. For a time he was unable to shift himself from his attachment to his earthly carcass. For a time this new strange cloud body of his simply swayed, contracted, expanded, coiled, and writhed with his efforts to free himself, and then quite suddenly the link that bound him snapped. For a moment everything was hidden by what appeared to be whirling spheres of dark vapour, and then through a momentary gap he saw his drooping body collapse limply, saw his lifeless head drop sideways, and found he was driving along like a huge cloud in a strange place of shadowy clouds that had the luminous intricacy of London spread like a model below.

But now he was aware that the fluctuating vapour about him was something more than vapour, and the temerarious excitement of his first essay was shot with fear. For he perceived, at first indistinctly, and then suddenly very clearly, that he was surrounded by *faces*! that each roll and coil of the seeming cloud-stuff was a face. And such faces! Faces of thin shadow, faces of gaseous tenuity. Faces like those faces that glare with intolerable strangeness upon the sleeper in the evil hours of his dreams. Evil, greedy eyes that were full of a covetous curiosity, faces with knit brows and snarling, smiling lips; their vague hands clutched at Mr. Bessel as he passed, and the rest of their bodies was but an elusive streak of trailing darkness. Never a word they said, never a sound from the mouths that seemed to gibber. All about him they pressed in that dreamy silence, passing freely through the dim mistiness that was his body, gathering ever more numerously about him. And the shadowy Mr. Bessel, now suddenly fear-stricken, drove through the silent, active multitude of eyes and clutching hands.

So inhuman were these faces, so malignant their staring eyes, and shadowy, clawing gestures, that it did not occur to Mr. Bessel to attempt intercourse with these drifting creatures. Idiot phantoms, they seemed, children of vain desire, beings unborn and forbidden the boon of being, whose only expressions and gestures told of the envy and craving for life that was their one link with existence.

It says much for his resolution that, amidst the swarming cloud of these noiseless spirits of evil, he could still think of Mr. Vincey. He made a violent effort of will and found himself, he knew not how, stooping towards Staple Inn, saw Vincey sitting attentive and alert in his arm-chair by the fire.

And clustering also about him, as they clustered ever about all that lives and breathes, was another multitude of these vain voiceless shadows, longing, desiring, seeking some loophole into life.

For a space Mr. Bessel sought ineffectually to attract his friend's attention. He tried to get in front of his eyes, to move the objects in his room, to touch him. But Mr. Vincey remained unaffected, ignorant of the being that was so close to his own. The strange something that Mr. Bessel has compared to a sheet of glass separated them impermeably.

And at last Mr. Bessel did a desperate thing. I have told how that in some strange way he could see not only the outside of a man as we see him, but within. He extended his shadowy hand and thrust his vague black fingers, as it seemed, through the heedless brain.

Then, suddenly, Mr. Vincey started like a man who

recalls his attention from wandering thoughts, and it seemed to Mr. Bessel that a little dark-red body situated in the middle of Mr. Vincey's brain swelled and glowed as he did so. Since that experience he has been shown anatomical figures of the brain, and he knows now that this is that useless structure, as doctors call it, the pineal eye. For, strange as it will seem to many, we have, deep in our brains—where it cannot possibly see any earthly light—an eye! At the time this, with the rest of the internal anatomy of the brain, was quite new to him. At the sight of its changed appearance, however, he thrust forth his finger, and, rather fearful still of the consequences, touched this little spot. And instantly Mr. Vincey started, and Mr. Bessel knew that he was seen.

And at that instant it came to Mr. Bessel that evil had happened to his body, and behold! a great wind blew through all that world of shadows and tore him away. So strong was this persuasion that he thought no more of Mr. Vincey, but turned about forthwith, and all the countless faces drove back with him like leaves before a gale. But he returned too late. In an instant he saw the body that he had left inert and collapsed—lying, indeed, like the body of a man just dead—had arisen by virtue of some strength and will beyond his own. It stood with staring eyes, stretching its limbs in dubious fashion.

For a moment he watched it in wild dismay, and then he stooped towards it. But the pane of glass had closed against him again, and he was foiled. He beat himself passionately against this, and all about him the spirits of evil grinned and pointed and mocked. He gave way to furious anger. He compares himself to a bird that has fluttered heedlessly into a room and is beating at the window-pane that holds it back from freedomt.

And behold! the little body that had once been his was now dancing with delight. He saw it shouting, though he could not hear its shouts; he saw the violence of its movements grow. He watched it fling his cherished furniture about in the mad delight of existence, rend his books apart, smash bottles, drink heedlessly from the jagged fragments, leap and smite in a passionate acceptance of living. He watched these actions in paralysed astonishment. Then once more he hurled himself against the impassable barrier, and then, with all that crew of mocking ghosts about him, hurried back in dire confusion to Vincey to tell him of the outrage that had come upon him.

But the brain of Vincey was now closed against apparitions, and the disembodied Mr..Bessel pursued him in vain as he hurried out into Holborn to call a cab. Foiled and terror-stricken, Mr. Bessel swept back again, to find his desecrated body whooping in a glorious frenzy down the Burlington Arcade. . . .

And now the attentive reader begins to understand Mr. Bessel's interpretation of the first part of this strange story. The being whose frantic rush through London had inflicted so much injury and disaster had indeed Mr. Bessel's body, but it was not Mr. Bessel. It was an evil spirit out of that strange world beyond existence, into which Mr. Bessel had so rashly ventured. For twenty hours it held possession of him, and for all those twenty hours the dispossessed spirit-body of Mr. Bessel was going to and fro in that unheard-of middle world of shadows seeking help in vain.

He spent many hours beating at the minds of Mr. Vincey and of his friend Mr. Hart. Each, as we know, he roused by his efforts. But the language that might convey his situation to these helpers across the gulf he did not know ; his feeble fingers groped vainly and powerlessly in their brains. Once, indeed, as we have already told, he was able to turn Mr. Vincey aside from his path so that he encountered the stolen body in its career, but he could not make him understand the thing that had happened : he was unable to draw any help from that encounter. . . .

All through those hours the persuasion was overwhelming in Mr. Bessel's mind that presently his body would be killed by its furious tenant, and he would have to remain in this shadow-land for evermore. So that those long hours were a growing agony of fear. And ever as he hurried to and fro in his ineffectual excitement, innumerable spirits of that world about him mobbed him and confused his mind. And ever an envious applauding multitude poured after their successful fellow as he went upon his glorious career.

For that, it would seem, must be the life of these bodiless things of this world that is the shadow of our world. Ever they watch, coveting a way into a mortal body, in order that they may descend, as furies and frenzies, as violent lusts and mad, strange impulses, rejoicing in the body they have won. For Mr. Bessel was not the only human soul in that place. Witness the fact that he met first one, and afterwards several shadows of men, men like himself, it seemed, who had lost their bodies even it may be as he had lost his, and wandered, despairingly, in that lost world that is neither life nor death. They could not speak because that world is silent, yet he knew them for men because of their dim human bodies, and because of the sadness of their faces.

But how they had come into that world he could not tell, nor where the bodies they had lost might be, whether they still raved about the earth, or whether they were closed for ever in death against return. That they were the spirits of the dead neither he nor I believe. But Doctor Wilson Paget thinks they are the rational souls of men who are lost in madness on the earth.

At last Mr. Bessel chanced upon a place where a little crowd of such disembodied silent creatures was gathered, and thrusting through them he saw below a brightly-lit room, and four or five quiet gentlemen and a woman, a stoutish woman dressed in black bombazine and sitting awkwardly in a chair with her head thrown back. He knew her from her portraits to be Mrs. Bullock, the medium. And he perceived that tracts and structures in her brain glowed and stirred as he had seen the pineal eye in the brain of Mr. Vincey glow. Thr light was very fitful ; sometimes it was a broad illumination, and sometimes merely a faint twilight spot, and it shifted slowly about her brain. She kept on talking and writing with one hand. And Mr. Bessel saw that the crowding shadows of men about him, and a great multitude of the shadow spirits of that shadow-land, were all striving and thrusting to touch the lighted regions of her brain. As one gained her brain or another was thrust away, her voice and the writing of her hand changed. So that what she said was disorderly and confused for the most part ; now a fragment of one soul's message, and now a fragment of another's, and now she babbled the insane fancies of the spirits of vain desire. Then Mr. Bessel understood that she spoke for the spirit that had touch of her, and he began to struggle very furiously towards her. But he was on the outside of the crowd and at that time he could not reach her, and at last growing anxious, he went away to find what had happened meanwhile to his body.

For a long time he went to and fro seeking it in vain and fearing that it must have been killed, and then he found it at the bottom of the shaft in Baker Street, writhing furiously and cursing with pain. Its leg and an arm and two ribs had been broken by its fall. Moreover, the evil spirit was angry because his time had been so short and because of the pain—making violent movements and casting his body about.

And at that Mr. Bessel returned with redoubled earnestness to the room where the *séance* was going on, and so soon as he had thrust himself within sight of the place, he saw one of the men who stood about the medium looking at his watch as if he meant that the *séance* should presently end. At that a great number of the shadows who had been striving turned away with gestures of despair. But the thought that the *séance* was almost over only made Mr. Bessel the more earnest, and he struggled so stoutly with his will against the others that presently he gained the woman's brain. It chanced that just at that moment it glowed very brightly, and in that instant she wrote the message that Doctor Wilson Paget preserved. And then the other shadows and the cloud of evil spirits about him had thrust Mr. Bessel away from her, and for all the rest of the *séance* he could regain her no more.

So he went back and watched through the long hours at the bottom of the shaft where the evil spirit lay in the stolen body it had maimed, writhing and cursing, and weeping and groaning, and learning the lesson of pain. And towards dawn the thing he had waited for happened, the brain glowed brightly and the evil spirit came out, and Mr. Bessel entered the body he had feared he should never enter again. As he did so, the silence—the brooding silence—ended ; he

heard the tumult of traffic and the voices of people overhead, and that strange world that is the shadow of our
world—the dark and silent shadows of ineffectual desire
and the shadows of lost men—vanished clean away.

He lay there for the space of about three hours before he
was found.   And in spite of the pain and suffering of his
wounds, and of the dim damp place in which he lay ; in
spite of the tears—wrung from him by his physical distress
—his heart was full of gladness to know that he was nevertheless back once more in the kindly world of men.

THE CRYSTAL EGG

THERE WAS, until a year ago, a little and very grimy-looking shop near Seven Dials, over which, in weather-worn yellow lettering, the name of " C. Cave, Naturalist and Dealer in Antiquities," was inscribed. The contents of its window were curiously variegated. They comprised some elephant tusks and an imperfect set of chessmen, beads and weapons, a box of eyes, two skulls of tigers and one human, several moth-eaten stuffed monkeys (one holding a lamp), an old-fashioned cabinet, a fly-blown ostrich egg, or so, some fishing-tackle, and an extraordinarily dirty, empty glass fish-tank. There was also, at the moment the story begins, a mass of crystal, worked into the shape of an egg and brilliantly polished. And at that two people who stood outside the window were looking, one of them a tall, thin clergyman, the other a black-bearded young man of dusky complexion and unobtrusive costume. The dusky young man spoke with eager gesticulation, and seemed anxious for his companion to purchase the article.

While they were there, Mr. Cave came into his shop, his beard still wagging with the bread and butter of his tea. When he saw these men and the object of their regard, his countenance fell. He glanced guiltily over his shoulder, and softly shut the door. He was a little old man, with pale face and peculiar watery blue eyes ; his hair was a dirty gray, and he wore a shabby blue frock-coat, an ancient silk hat, and carpet slippers very much down at heel. He remained watching the two men as they talked. The clergyman went deep into his trouser pocket, examined a handful of money, and showed his teeth in an agreeable smile. Mr. Cave seemed still more depressed when they came into the shop.

The clergyman, without any ceremony, asked the price of the crystal egg. Mr. Cave glanced nervously towards the door leading into the parlour, and said five pounds. The clergyman protested that the price was high, to his companion as well as to Mr. Cave—it was, indeed, very much more than Mr. Cave had intended to ask when he had stocked the article—and an attempt at bargaining ensued. Mr. Cave stepped to the shop door, and held it open. " Five pounds is my price," he said, as though he wished to save himself the trouble of unprofitable discussion. As he did so, the upper portion of a woman's face appeared above the blind in the glass upper panel of the door leading into the parlour, and stared curiously at the two customers. " Five pounds is my price," said Mr. Cave, with a quiver in his voice.

The swarthy young man had so far remained a spectator watching Cave keenly. Now he spoke. " Give him five pounds," he said. The clergyman glanced at him to see if he were in earnest, and when he looked at Mr. Cave again, he saw that the latter's face was white. " It's a lot of money," said the clergyman, and diving into his pocket, began counting his resources. He had little more than thirty shillings, and he appealed to his companion, with whom he seemed to be on terms of considerable intimacy. This gave Mr. Cave an opportunity of collecting his thoughts, and he began to explain in an agitated manner that the crystal was not, as a matter of fact, entirely free for sale. His two customers were naturally surprised at this, and inquired why he had not thought of that before he began to bargain. Mr. Cave became confused, but he stuck to his story, that the crystal was not in the market that afternoon, that a probable purchaser of it had already appeared. The two, treating this as an attempt to raise the price still further, made as if they would leave the shop. But at this point the parlour door opened, and the owner of the dark fringe and the little eyes appeared.

She was a coarse-featured, corpulent woman, younger and very much larger than Mr. Cave ; she walked heavily, and her face was flushed. " That crystal is for sale," she said. " And five pounds is a good enough price for it. I can't think what you're about, Cave, not to take the gentleman's offer ! "

Mr. Cave, greatly perturbed by the interruption, looked angrily at her over the rims of his spectacles, and without excessive assurance, asserted his right to manage his business in his own way. An altercation began. The two customers watched the scene with interest and some amusement, occasionally assisting Mrs. Cave with suggestions. Mr. Cave, hard driven, persisted in a confused and impossible story of an inquiry for the crystal that morning, and his agitation became painful. But he stuck to his point with extraordinary persistence. It was the young Oriental who ended this curious controversy. He proposed that they should call again in the course of two days—so as to give the alleged inquirer a fair chance. "And then we must insist," said the clergyman. "Five pounds." Mrs. Cave took it on herself to apologise for her husband, explaining that he was sometimes "a little odd," and as the two customers left, the couple prepared for a free discussion of the incident in all its bearings.

Mrs. Cave talked to her husband with singular directness The poor little man, quivering with emotion, muddled himself between his stories, maintaining on the one hand that he had another customer in view, and on the other asserting that the crystal was honestly worth ten guineas. "Why did you ask five pounds?" said his wife. "*Do* let me manage my business my own way!" said Mr. Cave.

Mr. Cave had living with him a stepdaughter and a stepson, and at supper that night the transaction was re-discussed. None of them had a high opinion of Mr. Cave's business methods, and this action seemed a culminating folly.

"It's my opinion he's refused that crystal before," said the stepson, a loose-limbed lout of eighteen.

"But *Five Pounds*!" said the stepdaughter, an argumentative young woman of six-and-twenty.

Mr. Cave's answers were wretched; he could only mumble weak assertions that he knew his own business best. They drove him from his half-eaten supper into the shop, to close it for the night, his ears aflame and tears of vexation behind his spectacles. Why had he left the crystal in the window so long? The folly of it! That was the trouble closest in his mind. For a time he could see no way of evading sale.

After supper his stepdaughter and stepson smartened themselves up and went out and his wife retired upstairs to reflect upon the business aspects of the crystal, over a little sugar and lemon and so forth in hot water. Mr. Cave went into the shop, and stayed there until late, ostensibly to make ornamental rockeries for gold-fish cases, but really for a private purpose that will be better explained later. The next day Mrs. Cave found that the crystal had been removed from the window, and was lying behind some second-hand books on angling. She replaced it in a conspicuous position. But she did not argue further about it, as a nervous headache disinclined her from debate. Mr. Cave was always disinclined. The day passed disagreeably. Mr. Cave was, if anything, more absent-minded than usual, and uncommonly irritable withal. In the afternoon, when his wife was taking her customary sleep, he removed the crystal from the window again.

The next day Mr. Cave had to deliver a consignment of dog-fish at one of the hospital schools, where they were needed for dissection. In his absence Mrs. Cave's mind reverted to the topic of the crystal, and the methods of expenditure suitable to a windfall of five pounds. She had already devised some very agreeable expedients, among others a dress of green silk for herself and a trip to Richmond, when a jangling of the front door bell summoned her into the shop. The customer was an examination coach who came to complain of the non-delivery of certain frogs asked for the previous day. Mrs. Cave did not approve of this particular branch of Mr. Cave's business, and the gentleman, who had called in a somewhat aggressive mood, retired after a brief exchange of words—entirely civil, so far as he was concerned. Mrs. Cave's eye then naturally turned to the window ; for the sight of the crystal was an assurance of the five pounds and of her dreams. What was her surprise to find it gone !

She went to the place behind the locker on the counter where she had discovered it the day before. It was not there ; and she immediately began an eager search about the shop.

When Mr. Cave returned from his business with the

dogfish, about a quarter to two in the afternoon, he found the shop in some confusion, and his wife, extremely exasperated and on her knees behind the counter, routing among his taxidermic material. Her face came up hot and angry over the counter, as the jangling bell announced his return, and she forthwith accused him of " hiding it."

" Hid *what* ? " asked Mr. Cave.

" The crystal ! "

At that Mr. Cave, apparently much surprised, rushed to the window. " Isn't it here ? " he said. " Great Heavens ! what has become of it ? "

Just then Mr. Cave's stepson re-entered the shop from the inner room—he had come home a minute or so before Mr. Cave—and he was blaspheming freely. He was apprenticed to a second-hand furniture dealer down the road, but he had his meals at home, and he was naturally annoyed to find no dinner ready.

But when he heard of the loss of the crystal, he forgot his meal, and his anger was diverted from his mother to his stepfather. Their first idea, of course, was that he had hidden it. But Mr. Cave stoutly denied all knowledge of its fate, freely offering his bedabbled affidavit in the matter —and at last worked up to the point of accusing, first his wife and then his stepson of having taken it with a view to a private sale. So began an exceedingly acrimonious and emotional discussion, which ended for Mrs. Cave in a peculiar nervous condition midway between hysterics and amuck, and caused the stepson to be half an hour late at the furniture establishment in the afternoon. Mr. Cave took refuge from his wife's emotions in the shop.

In the evening the matter was resumed, with less passion and in a judicial spirit, under the presidency of the stepdaughter. The supper passed unhappily and culminated in a painful scene. Mr. Cave gave way at last to extreme exasperation, and went out banging the front door violently. The rest of the family, having discussed him with the freedom his absence warranted, hunted the house from garret to cellar, hoping to light upon the crystal.

The next day the two customers called again. They were received by Mrs. Cave almost in tears. It transpired that no one *could* imagine all that she had stood from Cave at various times in her married pilgrimage.

. . . She also gave a garbled account of the disappearance. The clergyman and the Oriental laughed silently at one another, and said it was very extraordinary. As Mrs. Cave seemed disposed to give them the complete history of her life they made to leave the shop. Thereupon Mrs. Cave, still clinging to hope, asked for the clergyman's address, so that, if she could get anything out of Cave, she might communicate it. The address was duly given, but apparently was afterwards mislaid. Mrs. Cave can remember nothing about it.

In the evening of that day the Caves seem to have exhausted their emotions, and Mr. Cave, who had been out in the afternoon, supped in a gloomy isolation that contrasted pleasantly with the impassioned controversy of the previous days. For some time matters were very badly strained in the Cave household, but neither crystal nor customer reappeared.

Now, without mincing the matter, we must admit that Mr. Cave was a liar. He knew perfectly well where the crystal was. It was in the rooms of Mr. Jacoby Wace, Assistant Demonstrator at St. Catherine's Hospital, Westbourne Street. It stood on the sideboard partially covered by a black velvet cloth, and beside a decanter of American whisky. It is from Mr. Wace, indeed, that the particulars upon which this narrative is based were derived. Cave had taken off the thing to the hospital hidden in the dog-fish sack, and there had pressed the young investigator to keep it for him. Mr. Wace was a little dubious at first. His relationship to Cave was peculiar. He had a taste for singular characters, and he had more than once invited the old man to smoke and drink in his rooms, and to unfold his rather amusing views of life in general and of his wife in particular. Mr. Wace had encountered Mrs. Cave, too, on occasions when Mr. Cave was not at home to attend to him. He knew the constant interference to which Cave was subjected, and having weighed the story judicially, he decided to give the crystal a refuge. Mr. Cave promised to explain the reasons for his remarkable affection for the crystal more fully on a later occasion, but he spoke distinctly of seeing visions therein. He called on Mr. Wace the same evening.

He told a complicated story. The crystal he said had come into his possession with other oddments at the forced sale of another curiosity dealer's effects, and not knowing what its value might be, he had ticketed it at ten shillings. It had hung upon his hands at that price for some months, and he was thinking of "reducing the figure," when he made a singular discovery.

At that time his health was very bad—and it must be borne in mind that, throughout all this experience his physical condition was one of ebb—and he was in considerable distress by reason of the negligence, the positive ill-treatment even, he received from his wife and stepchildren. His wife was vain, extravagant, unfeeling, and had a growing taste for private drinking; his stepdaughter was mean and over-reaching; and his stepson had conceived a violent dislike for him, and lost no chance of showing it. The requirements of his business pressed heavily upon him, and Mr. Wace does not think that he was altogether free from occasional intemperance. He had begun life in a comfortable position, he was a man of fair education, and he suffered, for weeks at a stretch, from melancholia and insomnia. Afraid to disturb his family, he would slip quietly from his wife's side, when his thoughts became intolerable, and wander about the house. And about three o'clock one morning, late in August, chance directed him into the shop.

The dirty little place was impenetrably black except in one spot, where he perceived an unusual glow of light. Approaching this, he discovered it to be the crystal egg, which was standing on the corner of the counter towards the window. A thin ray smote through a crack in the shutters, impinged upon the object, and seemed as it were to fill its entire interior.

It occurred to Mr. Cave that this was not in accordance with the laws of optics as he had known them in his younger days. He could understand the rays being refracted by the crystal and coming to a focus in its interior, but this

162

diffusion jarred with his physical conceptions. He approached the crystal nearly, peering into it and round it, with a transient revival of the scientific curiosity that in his youth had determined his choice of a calling. He was surprised to find the light not steady, but writhing within the substance of the egg, as though that object was a hollow sphere of some luminous vapour. In moving about to get different points of view, he suddenly found that he had come between it and the ray, and that the crystal none the less remained luminous. Greatly astonished, he lifted it out of the light ray and carried it to the darkest part of the shop. It remained bright for some four or five minutes, when it slowly faded and went out. He placed it in the thin streak of daylight, and its luminousness was almost immediately restored.

So far, at least, Mr. Wace was able to verify the remarkable story of Mr. Cave. He has himself repeatedly held this crystal in a ray of light (which had to be of a less diameter than one millimeter). And in a perfect darkness, such as could be produced by velvet wrapping, the crystal did undoubtedly appear very faintly phosphorescent. It would seem, however, that the luminousness was of some exceptional sort, and not equally visible to all eyes ; for Mr. Harbinger—whose name will be familiar to the scientific reader in connection with the Pasteur Institute—was quite unable to see any light whatever. And Mr. Wace's own capacity for its appreciation was out of comparison inferior to that of Mr. Cave's. Even with Mr. Cave the power varied very considerably ; his vision was most vivid during states of extreme weakness and fatigue.

Now, from the outset, this light in the crystal exercised a curious fascination upon Mr. Cave. And it says more for his loneliness of soul than a volume of pathetic writing could do, that he told no human being of his curious observations. He seems to have been living in such an atmosphere of petty spite that to admit the existence of a pleasure would have been to risk the loss of it. He found that as the dawn advanced, and the amount of diffused light increased, the crystal became to all appearance non-luminous. And for some time he was unable to see anything in it, except at night-time, in dark corners of the shop.

But the use of an old velvet cloth, which he used as a background for a collection of minerals, occurred to him, and by doubling this, and putting it over his head and hands, he was able to get a sight of the luminous movement within the crystal even in the day-time. He was very cautious lest he should be thus discovered by his wife, and he practised this occupation only in the afternoons, while she was asleep upstairs, and then circumspectly in a hollow under the counter.

And one day, turning the crystal about in his hands, he saw something. It came and went like a flash, but it gave him the impression that the object had for a moment opened to him the view of a wide and spacious and strange country; and turning it about, he did, just as the light faded, see the same vision again.

Now it would be tedious and unnecessary to state all the phases of Mr. Cave's discovery from this point. Suffice that the effect was this : the crystal, being peered into at an angle of about 137 degrees from the direction of the illuminating ray, gave a clear and consistent picture of a wide and peculiar countryside. It was not dream-like at all : it produced a definite impression of reality, and the better the light the more real and solid it seemed. It was a moving picture : that is to say, certain objects moved in it, but slowly in an orderly manner like real things, and, according as the direction of the lighting and vision changed, the picture changed also. It must, indeed, have been like looking through an oval glass at a view, and turning the glass about to get at different aspects.

Mr. Cave's statements, Mr. Wace assures me, were extremely circumstantial, and entirely free from any of that emotional quality that taints hallucinatory impressions. But it must be remembered that all the efforts of Mr. Wace to see any similar clarity in the faint opalescence of the crystal were wholly unsuccessful, try as he would. The difference in intensity of the impressions received by the two men was very great, and it is quite conceivable that what was a view to Mr. Cave was a mere blurred nebulosity to Mr. Wace.

The view, as Mr. Cave described it, was invariably of an extensive plain, and he seemed always to be looking at it from a considerable height, as if from a tower or a mast. To the east and to the west the plain was bounded at a remote distance by vast reddish cliffs, which reminded him of those he had seen in some picture : but what the picture was Mr. Wace was unable to ascertain. These cliffs passed north and south—he could tell the points of the compass by the stars that were visible of a night—receding in an almost illimitable perspective and fading into the mists of the distance before they met. He was nearer the eastern set of cliffs ; on the occasion of his first vision the sun was rising over them, and black against the sunlight and pale against their shadow appeared a multitude of soaring forms that Mr. Cave regarded as birds. A vast range of buildings spread below him ; he seemed to be looking down upon them ; and as they approached the blurred and refracted edge of the picture they became indistinct. There were also trees curious in shape, and in colouring a deep mossy green and an exquisite gray, beside a wide and shining canal. And something great and brilliantly coloured flew across the picture. But the first time Mr. Cave saw these pictures he saw only in flashes, his hands shook, his head moved, the vision came and went, and grew foggy and indistinct. And at first he had the greatest difficulty in finding the picture again once the direction of it was lost.

His next clear vision, which came about a week after the first, the interval having yielded nothing but tantalising glimpses and some useful experience, showed him the view down the length of the valley. The view was different, but he had a curious persuasion, which his subsequent observations abundantly confirmed, that he was regarding the strange world from exactly the same spot, although he was looking in a different direction. The long façade of the great building, whose roof he had looked down upon before, was now receding in perspective. He recognised the roof. In the front of the façade was a terrace of massive proportions and extraordinary length, and down the middle of the terrace, at certain intervals, stood huge but very graceful masts, bearing small shiny objects which reflected the setting sun. The import of these small objects did not occur to Mr. Cave until some time after, as he was describing the scene to Mr. Wace. The terrace overhung a thicket of the must luxuriant and graceful vegetation, and beyond this was a wide grassy lawn on which certain broad creatures, in form like beetles but enormously larger, reposed. Beyond this again was a richly decorated causeway of pinkish stone ; and beyond that, and lined with dense red weeds, and passing up the valley exactly parallel with the distant cliffs, was a broad and mirror-like expanse of water. The air seemed full of squadrons of great birds, manoeuvring in stately curves ; and across the river was a multitude of splendid buildings, richly coloured and glittering with metallic tracery and facets, among a forest of moss-like and lichenous trees. And suddenly something flapped repeatedly across the vision, like the fluttering of a jewelled fan or the beating of a wing, and a face, or rather the upper part of a face with very large eyes, came, as it were, close to his own and as if on the other side of the crystal. Mr. Cave was so startled and so impressed by the absolute reality of these eyes that he drew his head back from the crystal to look behind it. He had become so absorbed in watching that he was quite surprised to find himself in the cool darkness of his little shop, with its familiar odour of methyl, mustiness, and decay. And as he blinked about him, the glowing crystal faded and went out.

Such were the first general impressions of Mr. Cave. The story is curiously direct and circumstantial. From the outset, when the valley first flashed momentarily on his senses, his imagination was strangely affected, and as he began to appreciate the details of the scene he saw, his wonder rose to the point of a passion. He went about his business listless and distraught, thinking only of the time when he should be able to return to his watching. And then a few weeks after his first sight of the valley came the two customers, the stress and excitement of their offer, and the narrow escape of the crystal from sale, as I have already told.

Now, while the thing was Mr. Cave's secret, it remained

a mere wonder, a thing to creep to covertly and peep at, as a child might peep upon a forbidden garden. But Mr. Wace has, for a young scientific investigator, a particularly lucid and consecutive habit of mind. Directly the crystal and its story came to him, and he had satisfied himself, by seeing the phosphorescence with his own eyes, that there really was a certain evidence for Mr. Cave's statements, he proceeded to develop the matter systematically. Mr. Cave was only too eager to come and feast his eyes on this wonderland he saw, and he came every night from half-past eight until half-past ten, and sometimes, in Mr. Wace's absence during the day. On Sunday afternoons, also, he came. From the outset Mr. Wace made copious notes, and it was due to his scientific method that the relation between the direction from which the initiating ray entered the crystal and the orientation of the picture were proved. And, by covering the crystal in a box perforated only with a small aperture to admit the exciting ray, and by substituting black holland for his buff blinds, he greatly improved the conditions of the observations; so that in a little while they were able to survey the valley in any direction they desired.

So having cleared the way, we may give a brief account of this visionary world within the crystal. The things were in all cases seen by Mr. Cave, and the method of working was invariably for him to watch the crystal and report what he saw, while Mr. Wace (who as a science student had learnt the trick of writing in the dark) wrote a brief note of his report. When the crystal faded, it was put into its box in the proper position and the electric light turned on. Mr. Wace asked questions, and suggested observations to clear up difficult points. Nothing, indeed, could have been less visionary and more matter-of-fact.

The attention of Mr. Cave had been speedily directed to the bird-like creatures he had seen so abundantly present in each of his earlier visions. His first impression was soon corrected, and he considered for a time that they might represent a diurnal species of bat. Then he thought, grotesquely enough, that they might be cherubs. Their heads were round and curiously human, and it was the eyes of one of them that had so startled him on his second observation. They had broad, silvery wings, not feathered, but glistening almost as brilliantly as new-killed fish and with the same subtle play of colour, and these wings were not built on the plan of bird-wing or bat, Mr. Wace learned, but supported by curved ribs radiating from the body. (A sort of butterfly wing with curved ribs seems best to express their appearance.) The body was small, but fitted with two bunches of prehensile organs, like long tentacles, immediately under the mouth. Incredible as it appeared to Mr. Wace, the persuasion at last became irresistible that it was these creatures which owned the great quasi-human buildings and the magnificent garden that made the broad valley so splendid. And Mr. Cave perceived that the buildings, with other peculiarities, had no doors, but that the great circular windows, which opened freely, gave the creatures egress and entrance. They would alight upon their tentacles, fold their wings to a smallness almost rod-like, and hop into the interior. But among them was a multitude of smaller-winged creatures, like great dragon-flies and moths and flying beetles, and across the greensward brilliantly-coloured gigantic ground-beetles crawled lazily to and fro. Moreover, on the causeways and terraces, large-headed creatures similar to the greater winged flies, but wingless, were visible, hopping busily upon their hand-like tangle of tentacles.

Allusion has already been made to the glittering objects upon masts that stood upon the terrace of the nearer building. It dawned upon Mr. Cave, after regarding one of these masts very fixedly on one particularly vivid day that the glittering object there was a crystal exactly like that into which he peered. And a still more careful scrutiny convinced him that each one in a vista of nearly twenty carried a similar object.

Occasionally one of the large flying creatures would flutter up to one, and folding its wings and coiling a number of its tentacles about the mast, would regard the crystal fixedly for a space—sometimes for as long as fifteen minutes. And a series of observations, made at the suggestion of Mr. Wace, convinced both watchers that, so far as this visionary world was concerned, the crystal into which they peered actually stood at the summit of the endmost mast on the terrace, and that on one occasion at least one of these inhabitants of this other world had looked into Mr. Cave's face while he was making these observations.

So much for the essential facts of this very singular story. Unless we dismiss it all as the ingenious fabrication of Mr. Wace, we have to believe one of two things : either that Mr. Cave's crystal was in two worlds at once, and that while it was carried about in one, it remained stationary in the other, which seems altogether absurd ; or else that it had some peculiar relation of sympathy with another and exactly similar crystal in this other world, so that what was seen in the interior of the one in this world was, under suitable conditions, visible to an observer in the corresponding crystal in the other world ; and *vice versa.* At present, indeed, we do not know of any way in which two crystals could so come *en rapport,* but nowadays we know enough to understand that the thing is not altogether impossible. This view of the crystals as *en rapport* was the supposition that occurred to Mr. Wace, and to me at least it seems extremely plausible. . . .

And where was this other world ? On this, also, the alert intelligence of Mr. Wave speedily threw light. After sunset, the sky darkened rapidly—there was a very brief twilight interval indeed—and the stars shone out. They were recognisably the same as those we see, arranged in the same constellations. Mr. Cave recognised the Bear, the Pleiades, Aldebaran, and Sirius ; so that the other world must be somewhere in the solar system, and, at the utmost, only a few hundreds of millions of miles from our own. Following up this clue, Mr. Wace learned that the midnight sky was a darker blue even than our midwinter sky, and that the sun seemed a little smaller. *And there were two small moons !* " like our moon but smaller, and quite differently marked," one of which moved so rapidly that its motion was clearly visible, as one regarded it. These moons were never high in the sky, but vanished as they rose : that is, every time they revolved they were eclipsed because they were so near their primary planet. And all this answers quite completely, although Mr. Cave did not know it, to what must be the condition of things on Mars.

Indeed, it seems an exceedingly plausible conclusion that peering into this crystal Mr. Cave did actually see the planet Mars and its inhabitants. And if that be the case, then the evening star that shone so brilliantly in the sky of that distant vision was neither more or less than our own familiar earth.

For a time the Martians—if they were Martians—do not seem to have known of Mr. Cave's inspection. Once or twice one would come to peer, and go away very shortly to some other mast, as though the vision was unsatisfactory. During this time Mr. Cave was able to watch the proceedings of these winged people without being disturbed by their attentions, and although his report is necessarily vague and fragmentary, it is nevertheless very suggestive. Imagine the impression of humanity a Martian observer would get who, after a difficult process of preparation and with considerable fatigue to the eyes, was able to peer at London from the steeple of St. Martin's Church for stretches, at longest, of four minutes at a time. Mr. Cave was unable to ascertain if the winged Martians were the same as the Martians who hopped about the causeways and terraces, and if the latter could put on wings at will. He several times saw certain clumsy bipeds, dimly suggestive of apes, white and partially translucent, feeding among certain of the lichenous trees, and once some of these fled before one of the hopping, round-headed Martians. The latter caught one in its tentacles, and then the picture faded suddenly and left Mr. Cave most tantalisingly in the dark. On another occasion a vast thing, that Mr. Cave thought at first was some gigantic insect, appeared advancing along the causeway beside the canal with extraordinary rapidity. As this drew nearer Mr. Cave perceived that it was a mechanism of shining metals and of extraordinary complexity. And then, when he looked again, it had passed out of sight.

After a time Mr. Wace aspired to attract the attention of the Martians, and the next time that the strange eyes of one of them appeared close to the crystal Mr. Cave cried out and sprang away, and they immediately turned on the light and began to gesticulate in a manner suggestive of signalling.

But when at last Mr. Cave examined the crystal again the Martian had departed.

Thus far these observations had progressed in early November, and then Mr. Cave, feeling that the suspicions of his family about the crystal were allayed, began to take it to and fro with him in order that, as occasion arose in the daytime or night, he might comfort himself with what was fast becoming the most real thing in his existence.

In December Mr. Wace's work in connection with a forthcoming examination became heavy, the sittings were reluctantly suspended for a week, and for ten or eleven days —he is not quite sure which—he saw nothing of Cave. He then grew anxious to resume these investigations, and, the stress of his seasonal labours being abated, he went down to Seven Dials. At the corner he noticed a shutter before a bird fancier's window and then another at a cobbler's. Mr. Cave's shop was closed.

He rapped and the door was opened by the stepson in black. He at once called Mrs. Cave, who was, Mr. Wace could not but observe, in cheap but ample widow's weeds of the most imposing pattern. Without any very great surprise Mr. Wace learnt that Cave was dead and already buried. She was in tears, and her voice was a little thick. She had just returned from Highgate. Her mind seemed occupied with her own prospects and the honourable details of the obsequies, but Mr. Wace was at last able to learn of the particulars of Cave's death. He had been found dead in his shop in the early morning, the day after his last visit to Mr. Wace, and the crystal had been clasped in his stone-cold hands. His face was smiling, said Mrs. Cave, and the velvet cloth from the minerals lay on the floor at his feet. He must have been dead five or six hours when he was found.

This came as a great shock to Wace, and he began to reproach himself bitterly for having neglected the plain symptoms of the old man's ill-health. But his chief thought was of the crystal. He approached that topic in a gingerly manner, because he knew Mrs. Cave's peculiarities. He was dumbfounded to learn that it was sold.

Mrs. Cave's first impulse, directly Cave's body had been taken upstairs, had been to write to the mad clergyman who had offered five pounds for the crystal, informing him of its recovery ; but after a violent hunt, in which her daughter joined her, they were convinced of the loss of his address. As they were without the means required to mourn and bury Cave in the elaborate style the dignity of an old Seven Dials inhabitant demands, they had appealed to a friendly fellow-tradesman in Great Portland Street. He had very kindly taken over a portion of the stock at a valuation. The valuation was his own, and the crystal egg was included in one of the lots. Mr. Wace, after a few suitable condolences, a little offhandedly proffered perhaps, hurried at once to Great Portland Street. But there he learned that the crystal egg had already been sold to a tall, dark man in gray. And there the material facts in this curious, and to me at least very suggestive, story come abruptly to an end. The Great Portland Street dealer did not know who the tall dark man in gray was, nor had he observed him with sufficient attention to describe him minutely. He did not even know which way this person had gone after leaving the shop. For a time Mr. Wace remained in the shop, trying the dealer's patience with hopeless questions, venting his own exasperation. And at last, realising abruptly that the whole thing had passed out of his hands, had vanished like a vision of the night, he returned to his own rooms, a little astonished to find the notes he had made still tangible and visible upon his untidy table.

His annoyance and disappointment were naturally very great. He made a second call (equally ineffectual) upon the Great Portland Street dealer, and he resorted to advertisements in such periodicals as were likely to come into the hands of a *bric-a-brac* collector. He also wrote letters to *The Daily Chronicle* and *Nature*, but both those periodicals, suspecting a hoax, asked him to reconsider his action before they printed, and he was advised that such a strange story, unfortunately so bare of supporting evidence, might imperil his reputation as an investigator. Moreover, the calls of his proper work were urgent. So that after a month or so, save for an occasional reminder to certain dealers, he had reluctantly to abandon the quest for the crystal egg, and from that day to this it remains undiscovered. Occasionally, however, he tells me, and I can quite believe him, he has bursts of zeal, in which he abandons his more urgent occupation and resumes the search.

Whether or not it will remain lost for ever, with the material and origin of it, are things equally speculative at the present time. If the present purchaser is a collecter, one would have expected the inquiries of Mr. Wace to have reached him through the dealers. He has been able to discover Mr. Cave's clergyman and " Oriental "—no other than the Rev. James Parker and the young Prince of Bosso-Kuni in Java. I am obliged to them for certain particulars. The object of the Prince was simply curiosity—and extravagance. He was so eager to buy because Cave was so oddly reluctant to sell. It is just as possible that the buyer in the second instance was simply a casual purchaser, and not a collector at all, and the crystal egg, for all I know, may at the present moment be within a mile of me, decorating a drawing-room or serving as a paper-weight—its remarkable functions all unknown. Indeed, it is partly with the idea of such a possibility that I have thrown this narrative into a form that will give it a chance of being read by the ordinary consumer of fiction.

My own ideas in the matter are practically identical with those of Mr. Wace. I believe the crystal on the mast in Mars and the crystal egg of Mr. Cave's to be in some physical, but at present quite inexplicable, way *en rapport*, and we both believe further that the terrestial crystal must have been—possibly at some remote date—sent hither from that planet, in order to give the Martians a near view of our affairs. Possibly the fellows to the crystals on the other masts are also on our globe. No theory of hallucination suffices for the facts.

THE DOOR IN THE WALL

I

ONE CONFIDENTIAL evening, not three months ago, Lionel Wallace told me this story of the Door in the Wall. And at the time I thought that so far as he was concerned it was a true story.

He told it me with such a direct simplicity of conviction that I could not do otherwise than believe in him. But in the morning, in my own flat, I woke to a different atmosphere, and as I lay in bed and recalled the things he had told me, stripped of the glamour of his earnest slow voice, denuded of the focused, shaded table light, the shadowy atmosphere that wrapped about him and me, and the pleasant bright things, the dessert and glasses and napery of the dinner we had shared, making them for the time a bright little world quite cut off from everyday realities, I saw it all as frankly incredible. " He was mystifying ! " I said, and then : " How well he did it ! . . . It isn't quite the thing I should have expected him, of all people, to do well."

Afterwards as I sat up in bed and sipped my morning tea, I found myself trying to account for the flavour of reality that perplexed me in his impossible reminiscences, by supposing they did in some way suggest, present, convey —I hardly know which word to use—experiences it was otherwise impossible to tell.

Well, I don't resort to that explanation now. I have got over my intervening doubts. I believe now, as I believed at the moment of telling, that Wallace did to the very best of his ability strip the truth of his secret for me. But whether he himself saw, or only thought he saw, whether he himself was the possessor of an inestimable privilege or the victim of a fantastic dream, I cannot pretend to guess. Even the facts of his death, which ended my doubts for ever, throw no light on that.

That much the reader must judge for himself.

I forget now what chance comment or criticism of mine moved so reticent a man to confide in me. He was, I think, defending himself against an imputation of slackness and unreliability I had made in relation to a great public movement, in which he had disappointed me. But he plunged suddenly. "I have," he said, "a preoccupation——"

"I know," he went on, after a pause, "I have been negligent. The fact is—it isn't a case of ghosts or apparitions—but—it's an odd thing to tell of, Redmond—I am haunted. I am haunted by something—that rather takes the light out of things, that fills me with longings . . ."

He paused, checked by that English shyness that so often overcomes us when we would speak of moving or grave or beautiful things. "You were at Saint Aethelstan's all through," he said, and for a moment that seemed to me quite irrelevant. "Well"—and he paused. Then very haltingly at first, but afterwards more easily, he began to tell of the thing that was hidden in his life, the haunting memory of a beauty and a happiness that filled his heart with insatiable longings, that made all the interests and spectacle of worldly life seem dull and tedious and vain to him.

Now that I have the clue to it, the thing seems written visibly in his face. I have a photograph in which that look of detachment has been caught and intensified. It reminds me of what a woman once said of him—a woman who had loved him greatly. "Suddenly," she said, "the interest goes out of him. He forgets you. He doesn't care a rap for you—under his very nose . . ."

Yet the interest was not always out of him, and when he was holding his attention to a thing, Wallace could contrive to be an extremely successful man. His career, indeed, is set with successes. He left me behind him long ago : he soared up over my head, and cut a figure in the world that I couldn't cut—anyhow. He was still a year short of forty, and they say now that he would have been in office and very probably in the new Cabinet if he had lived. At school he always beat me without effort—as it were by nature. We were at school together at Saint

Aethelstan's College in West Kensington for almost all our school-time. He came into the school as my co-equal, but he left far above me, in a blaze of scholarships and brilliant performance. Yet I think I made a fair average running. And it was at school I heard first of the "Door in the Wall"—that I was to hear of a second time only a month before his death.

To him at least the Door in the Wall was a real door, leading through a real wall to immortal realities. Of that I am now quite assured.

And it came into his life quite early, when he was a little fellow between five and six. I remember how, as he sat making his confession to me with a slow gravity, he reasoned and reckoned the date of it. "There was," he said, "a crimson Virginia creeper in it—all one bright uniform crimson, in a clear amber sunshine against a white wall. That came into the impression somehow, though I don't clearly remember how, and there were horse-chestnut leaves upon the clean pavement outside the green door. They were blotched yellow and green, you know, not brown nor dirty, so that they must have been new fallen. I take it that means October. I look out for horse-chestnut leaves every year and I ought to know.

"If I'm right in that, I was about five years and four months old."

He was, he said, rather a precocious little boy—he learnt to talk at an abnormally early age, and he was so sane and "old-fashioned," as people say, that he was permitted an amount of initiative that most children scarcely attain by seven or eight. His mother died when he was two, and he was under the less vigilant and authoritative care of a nursery governess. His father was a stern, preoccupied lawyer, who gave him little attention, and expected great things of him. For all his brightness he found life a little grey and dull, I think. And one day he wandered.

He could not recall the particular neglect that enabled him to get away, nor the course he took among the West Kensington roads. All that had faded among the incurable blurs of memory. But the white wall and the green door stood out quite distinctly.

As his memory of that childish experience ran, he did at the very first sight of that door experience a peculiar emotion, an attraction, a desire to get to the door and open it and walk in. And at the same time he had the clearest conviction that either it was unwise or it was wrong of him—he could not tell which—to yield to this attraction. He insisted upon it as a curious thing that he knew from the very beginning—unless memory has played him the queerest trick—that the door was unfastened, and that he could go in as he chose.

I seem to see the figure of that little boy, drawn and repelled. And it was very clear in his mind, too, though why it should be so was never explained, that his father would be very angry if he went in through that door.

Wallace described all these moments of hesitation to me with the utmost particularity. He went right past the door, and then, with his hands in his pockets and making an infantile attempt to whistle, strolled right along beyond the end of the wall. There he recalls a number of mean dirty shops, and particularly that of a plumber and decorator with a dusty disorder of earthenware pipes, sheet lead, ball taps, pattern books of wall paper, and tins of enamel. He stood pretending to examine these things, and *coveting*, passionately desiring, the green door.

Then, he said, he had a gust of emotion. He made a run for it, lest hesitation should grip him again ; he went plump with outstretched hand through the green door and let it slam behind him. And so, in a trice, he came into the garden that has haunted all his life.

It was very difficult for Wallace to give me his full sense of that garden into which he came.

There was something in the very air of it that exhilarated, that gave one a sense of lightness and good happening and well-being ; there was something in the sight of it that made all its colour clean and perfect and subtly luminous. In the instant of coming into it one was exquisitely glad— as only in rare moments, and when one is young and joyful one can be glad in this world. And everything was beautiful there. . . .

Wallace mused before he went on telling me. " You

see," he said, with the doubtful inflection of a man who pauses at incredible things, " there were two great panthers there. . . . Yes, spotted panthers. And I was not afraid. There was a long wide path with marble-edged flower borders on either side, and these two huge velvety beasts were playing there with a ball. One looked up and came towards me, a little curious as it seemed. It came right up to me, rubbed its soft round ear very gently against the small hand I held out, and purred. It was, I tell you, an enchanted garden. I know. And the size? Oh! it stretched far and wide, this way and that. I believe there were hills far away. Heaven knows where West Kensington had suddenly got to. And somehow it was just like coming home.

" You know, in the very moment the door swung to behind me, I forgot the road with its fallen chestnut leaves, its cabs and tradesmen's carts, I forgot the sort of gravitational pull back to the discipline and obedience of home, I forgot all hesitations and fear, forgot discretion, forgot all the intimate realities of this life. I became in a moment a very glad and wonder-happy little boy—in another world. It was a world with a different quality, a warmer, more penetrating and mellower light, with a faint clear gladness in its air, and wisps of sun-touched cloud in the blueness of its sky. And before me ran this long wide path, invitingly, with weedless beds on either side, rich with untended flowers, and these two great panthers. I put my little hands fearlessly on their soft fur, and caressed their round ears and the sensitive corners under their ears, and played with them, and it was as though they welcomed me home. There was a keen sense of home-coming in my mind, and when presently a tall, fair girl appeared in the pathway and came to meet me, smiling, and said 'Well?' to me, and lifted me, and kissed me, and put me down, and led me by the hand, there was no amazement, but only an impression of delightful rightness, of being reminded of happy things that had in some strange way been overlooked. There were broad red steps, I remember, that came into view between spikes of delphinium, and up these we went to a great avenue between very old and shady dark trees.

All down this avenue, you know, between the red chapped stems, were marble seats of honour and statuary, and very tame and friendly white doves . . .

" Along this cool avenue my girl-friend led me, looking down—I recall the pleasant lines, the finely-modelled chin of her sweet kind face—asking me questions in a soft, agreeable voice, and telling me things, pleasant things I know, though what they were I was never able to recall. . . . Presently a little Capuchin monkey, very clean, with a fur of ruddy brown and kindly hazel eyes, came down a tree to us and ran beside me, looking up at me and grinning, and presently leapt to my shoulder. So we two went on our way in great happiness."

He paused.

" Go on," I said.

" I remember little things. We passed an old man musing among laurels, I remember, and a place gay with paroquets, and came through a broad shaded colonnade to a spacious cool palace, full of pleasant fountains, full of beautiful things, full of the quality and promise of heart's desire. And there were many things and many people some that still seem to stand out clearly and some that are a little vague ; but all these people were beautiful and kind. In some way—I don't know how—it was conveyed to me that they all were kind to me, glad to have me there, and filling me with gladness by their gestures, by the touch of their hands, by the welcome and love in their eyes. Yes——"

He mused for a while. " Playmates I found there. That was very much to me, because I was a lonely little boy. They played delightful games in a grass-covered court, where there was a sun-dial set about with flowers. And as one played one loved. . . .

" But—it's odd—there's a gap in my memory. I don't remember the games we played. I never remembered. Afterwards, as a child, I spent long hours trying, even with tears, to recall the form of that happiness. I wanted to play it all over again—in my nursery—by myself. No ! All I remember is the happiness and two dear playfellows who were most with me. . . . Then presently came a sombre dark woman, with a grave, pale face, and dreamy eyes, a sombre woman, wearing a soft long robe of pale purple, who carried a book, and beckoned and took me aside with her into a gallery above a hall—though my playmates were loath to have me go, and ceased their game and stood watching as I was carried away. ' Come back to us ! ' they cried. ' Come back to us soon ! ' I looked up at her face, but she heeded them not at all. Her face was very gentle and grave. She took me to a seat in the gallery, and I stood beside her, ready to look at her book as she opened it upon her knee. The pages fell open. She pointed, and I looked, marvelling, for in the living pages of that book I saw myself ; it was a story about myself, and in it were all the things that had happened to me since ever I was born. . . .

" It was wonderful to me, because the pages of that book were not pictures, you understand, but realities."

Wallace paused gravely—looked at me doubtfully.

" Go on," I said. " I understand."

" They were realities—yes, they must have been ; people moved and things came and went in them ; my dear mother, whom I had near forgotten ; then my father, stern and upright, the servants, the nursery, all the familiar things of home. Then the front door and the busy streets, with traffic to and fro. I looked and marvelled, and looked half-doubtfully again into the woman's face and turned the pages over, skipping this and that, to see more of this book and more, and so at last I came to myself hovering and hesitating outside the green door in the long white wall, and felt again the conflict and the fear.

" ' And next ? ' I cried, and would have turned on, but the cool hand of the grave woman delayed me.

" ' Next ? ' I insisted, and struggled gently with her hand, pulling up her fingers with all my childish strength, and as she yielded and the page came over she bent down upon me like a shadow and kissed my brow.

" But the page did not show the enchanted garden, nor the panthers, nor the girl who had led me by the hand, nor the playfellows who had been so loath to let me go. It showed a long grey street in West Kensington, in that chill hour of afternoon before the lamps are lit, and I was there, a wretched little figure, weeping aloud, for all that I could do to restrain myself, and I was weeping because I could not return to my dear playfellows who had called after me, 'Come back to us! Come back to us soon!' I was there. This was no page in a book, but harsh reality; that enchanted place and the restraining hand of the grave mother at whose knee I stood had gone—whither had they gone?"

He halted again, and remained for a time staring into the fire.

"Oh! the woefulness of that return!" he murmured.

"Well?" I said, after a minute or so.

"Poor little wretch I was!—brought back to this gray world again! As I realised the fullness of what had happened to me, I gave way to quite ungovernable grief. And the shame and humiliation of that public weeping and my disgraceful home-coming remain with me still. I see again the benevolent-looking old gentleman in gold spectacles who stopped and spoke to me—prodding me first with his umbrella. 'Poor little chap,' said he; 'and are you lost then?'—and me a London boy of five and more! And he must needs bring in a kindly young policeman and make a crowd of me, and so march me home. Sobbing, conspicuous, and frightened, I came back from the enchanted garden to the steps of my father's house.

"That is as well as I can remember my vision of that garden—the garden that haunts me still. Of course, I can convey nothing of that indescribable quality of translucent unreality, that *difference* from the common things of experience that hung about it all; but that—that is what happened. If it was a dream, I am sure it was a daytime and altogether extraordinary dream. . . . H'm!—naturally there followed a terrible questioning, by my aunt, my father, the nurse, the governess—everyone. . . .

"I tried to tell them, and my father gave me my first thrashing for telling lies. When afterwards I tried to tell my aunt, she punished me again for my wicked persistence. Then, as I said, everyone was forbidden to listen to me, to hear a word about it. Even my fairy-tale books were taken

away from me for a time—because I was too ' imaginative.'
Eh? Yes, they did that! My father belonged to the old
school. . . . And my story was driven back upon myself.
I whispered it to my pillow—my pillow that was often
damp and salt to my whispering lips with childish tears.
And I added always to my official and less fervent prayers
this one heartfelt request : ' Please God I may dream of
the garden. Oh! take me back to my garden!' Take
me back to my garden! I dreamt often of the garden.
I may have added to it, I may have changed it ; I do not
know. . . . All this, you understand, is an attempt to recon-
struct from fragmentary memories a very early experience.
Between that and the other consecutive memories of my
boyhood there is a gulf. A time came when it seemed
impossible I should ever speak of that wonder glimpse
again."

I asked an obvious question.

" No," he said. " I don't remember that I ever attempted
to find my way back to the garden in those early years.
This seems odd to me now, but I think that very probably
a closer watch was kept on my movements after this mis-
adventure to prevent my going astray. No, it wasn't till
you knew me that I tried for the garden again. And I
believe there was a period—incredible as it seems now—
when I forgot the garden altogether—when I was about
eight or nine it may have been. Do you remember me as
a kid at Saint Aethelstan's ? "

" Rather ! "

" I didn't show any signs, did I, in those days of having
a secret dream ? "

2

He looked up with a sudden smile.
" Did you ever play North-West Passage with me ? . . .
No, of course you didn't come my way ! "
" It was the sort of game," he went on, " that every
imaginative child plays all day. The idea was the dis-
covery of a North-West Passage to school. The way to

school was plain enough ; the game consisted in finding some way that wasn't plain, starting off ten minutes early in some almost hopeless direction, and working my way round through unaccustomed streets to my goal. And one day I got entangled among some rather low-class streets on the other side of Campden Hill, and I began to think that for once the game would be against me and that I should get to school late. I tried rather desperately a street that seemed a *cul-de-sac*, and found a passage at the end. I hurried through that with renewed hope. ' I shall do it yet,' I said, and passed a row of frowsy little shops that were inexplicably familiar to me, and behold ! there was my long white wall and the green door that led to the enchanted garden !

" The thing whacked upon me suddenly. Then, after all, that garden, that wonderful garden, wasn't a dream ! "

He paused.

" I suppose my second experience with the green door marks the world of difference there is between the busy life of a schoolboy and the infinite leisure of a child. Anyhow, this second time I didn't for a moment think of going in straight away. You see—— For one thing, my mind was full of the idea of getting to school in time—set on not breaking my record for punctuality. I must surely have felt *some* little desire at least to try the door—yes. I must have felt that. . . . But I seem to remember the attraction of the door mainly as another obstacle to my overmastering determination to get to school. I was immensely interested by this discovery I had made, of course—I went on with my mind full of it—but I went on. It didn't check me. I ran past, tugging out my watch, found I had ten minutes still to spare, and then I was going downhill into familiar surroundings. I got to school, breathless, it is true and wet with perspiration, but in time. I can remember hanging up my coat and hat. . . . Went right by it and left it behind me. Odd, eh ? "

He looked at me thoughtfully. " Of course I didn't know then that it wouldn't always be there. Schoolboys have limited imaginations. I suppose I thought it was an awfully jolly thing to have it there, to know my way back to it, but there was the school tugging at me. I expect I was a good deal distraught and inattentive that morning, recalling what I could of the beautiful strange people I should presently see again. Oddly enough I had no doubt in my mind that they would be glad to see me. . . . Yes, I must have thought of the garden that morning just as a jolly sort of place to which one might resort in the interludes of a strenuous scholastic career.

" I didn't go that day at all. The next day was a half holiday, and that may have weighed with me. Perhaps, too, my state of inattention brought down impositions upon me, and docked the margin of time necessary for the detour. I don't know. What I do know is that in the meantime the enchanted garden was so much upon my mind that I could not keep it to myself.

" I told. What was his name ?—a ferrety-looking youngster we used to call Squiff."

" Young Hopkins," said I.

" Hopkins it was. I did not like telling him. I had a feeling that in some way it was against the rules to tell him, but I did. He was walking part of the way home with me ; he was talkative, and if we had not talked about the enchanted garden we should have talked of something else, and it was intolerable to me to think about any other subject. So I blabbed.

" Well, he told my secret. The next day in the play interval I found myself surrounded by half a dozen bigger boys, half teasing, and wholly curious to hear more of the enchanted garden. There was that big Fawcett—you remember him ?—and Carnaby and Morley Reynolds. You weren't there by any chance ? No, I think I should have remembered if you were. . . .

" A boy is a creature of odd feelings. I was, I really believe, in spite of my secret self-disgust, a little flattered to have the attention of these big fellows. I remember particularly a moment of pleasure caused by the praise of Crawshaw—you remember Crawshaw major, the son of Crawshaw the composer ?—who said it was the best lie he had ever heard. But at the same time there was a really painful undertow of shame at telling what I felt was indeed a sacred secret. That beast Fawcett made a joke about the girl in green——"

Wallace's voice sank with the keen memory of that shame. " I pretended not to hear," he said. " Well, then Carnaby suddenly called me a young liar, and disputed with me when I said the thing was true. I said I knew where to find the green door, could lead them all there in ten minutes. Carnaby became outrageously virtuous, and said I'd have to—and bear out my words or suffer. Did you ever have Carnaby twist your arm? Then perhaps you'll understand how it went with me. I swore my story was true. There was nobody in the school then to save a chap from Carnaby, though Crawshaw put in a word or so. Carnaby had got his game. I grew excited and red-eared, and a little frightened. I behaved altogether like a silly little chap, and the outcome of it all was that instead of starting alone for my enchanted garden, I led the way presently—cheeks flushed, ears hot, eyes smarting, and my soul one burning misery and shame—for a party of six mocking, curious, and threatening schoolfellows.

" We never found the white wall and the green door . . ."

" You mean——? "

" I mean I couldn't find it. I would have found it if I could.

" And afterwards when I could go alone I couldn't find it. I never found it. I seem now to have been always looking for it through my schoolboy days, but I never came upon it—never."

" Did the fellows—make it disagreeable? "

" Beastly. . . . Carnaby held a council over me for wanton lying. I remember how I sneaked home and upstairs to hide the marks of my blubbering. But when I cried myself to sleep at last it wasn't for Carnaby, but for the garden, for the beautiful afternoon I had hoped for, for the sweet friendly women and the waiting playfellows, and the game I had hoped to learn again, that beautiful forgotten game . . .

" I believed firmly that if I had not told— . . . I had bad times after that—crying at night and wool-gathering by day. For two terms I slackened and had bad reports.

Do you remember? Of course you would! It was *you*
—your beating me in mathematics that brought me back
to the grind again."

3

For a time my friend stared silently into the red heart of
the fire. Then he said : " I never saw it again until I was
seventeen.

" It leapt upon me for the third time—as I was driving
to Paddington on my way to Oxford and a scholarship,
I had just one momentary glimpse. I was leaning over
the apron of my hansom smoking a cigarette, and no doubt
thinking myself no end of a man of the world, and suddenly
there was the door, the wall, the dear sense of unforgettable
and still attainable things.

" We clattered by—I too taken by surprise to stop my
cab until we were well past and round a corner. Then I
had a queer moment, a double and divergent movement
of my will : I tapped the little door in the roof of the cab,
and brought my arm down to pull out my watch. ' Yes,
sir ! ' said the cabman, smartly. ' Er—well—it's nothing,'
I cried. ' *My* mistake ! We haven't much time ! Go
on ! ' And he went on. . . .

" I got my scholarship. And the night after I was told
of that, I sat over my fire in my little upper room, my study,
in my father's house, with his praise—his rare praise—and
his sound counsels ringing in my ears, and I smoked my
favourite pipe—the formidable bulldog of adolescence—
and thought of that door in the long white wall. ' If I had
stopped,' I thought, ' I should have missed my scholarship,
I should have missed Oxford—muddled all the fine career
before me ! I begin to see things better ! ' I fell musing
deeply, but I did not doubt then this career of mine was a
thing that merited sacrifice.

" Those dear friends and that clear atmosphere seemed
very sweet to me, very fine but remote. My grip was fixing
now upon the world. I saw another door opening—the
door of my career."

He stared again into the fire. Its red light picked out a stubborn strength in his face for just one flickering moment, and then it vanished again.

"Well," he said and sighed, "I have served that career. I have done—much work, much hard work. But I have dreamt of the enchanted garden a thousand dreams, and seen its door, or at least glimpsed its door, four times since then. Yes—four times. For a while this world was so bright and interesting, seemed so full of meaning and opportunity, that the half-effaced charm of the garden was by comparison gentle and remote. Who wants to pat panthers on the way to dinner with pretty women and distinguished men? I came down to London from Oxford, a man of bold promise that I have done something to redeem. Something—and yet there have been disappointments. . . .

"Twice I have been in love—I will not dwell on that—but once, as I went to someone who, I knew, doubted whether I dared to come, I took a short cut at a venture through an unfrequented road near Earl's Court, and so happened on a white wall and a familiar green door. 'Odd!' said I to myself, 'but I thought this place was on Campden Hill. It's the place I never could find somehow—like counting Stonehenge—the place of that queer daydream of mine.' And I went by it intent upon my purpose. It had no appeal to me that afternoon.

"I had just a moment's impulse to try the door, three steps aside were needed at the most—though I was sure enough in my heart that it would open to me—and then I thought that doing so might delay me on the way to that appointment in which I thought my honour was involved. Afterwards I was sorry for my punctuality— I might at least have peeped in, I thought, and waved a hand to those panthers, but I knew enough by this time not to seek again belatedly that which is not found by seeking. Yes, that time made me very sorry. . . .

"Years of hard work after that, and never a sight of the door. It's only recently it has come back to me. With it there has come a sense as though some thin tarnish had spread itself over my world. I began to think of it as a sorrowful and bitter thing that I should never see that door again. Perhaps I was suffering a little from overwork—perhaps it was what I've heard spoken of as the feeling of forty. I don't know. But certainly the keen brightness that makes effort easy has gone out of things recently, and that just at a time—with all these new political developments—when I ought to be working. Odd, isn't it? But I do begin to find life toilsome, its rewards, as I come near them, cheap. I began a little while ago to want the garden quite badly. Yes—and I've seen it three times."

"The garden?"

"No—the door! And I haven't gone in!"

He leant over the table to me, with an enormous sorrow in his voice as he spoke. "Thrice I have had my chance—*thrice*! If ever that door offers itself to me again, I swore, I will go in, out of this dust and heat, out of this dry glitter of vanity, out of these toilsome futilities. I will go and never return. This time I will stay. . . . I swore it, and when the time came—*I didn't go*.

"Three times in one year have I passed that door and failed to enter. Three times in the last year.

"The first time was on the night of the snatch division on the Tenant's Redemption Bill, on which the Government was saved by a majority of three. You remember? No one on our side—perhaps very few on the opposite side —expected the end that night. Then the debate collapsed like eggshells. I and Hotchkiss were dining with his cousin at Brentford; we were both unpaired, and we were called up by telephone, and set off at once in his cousin's motor. We got in barely in time, and on the way we passed my wall and door—livid in the moonlight, blotched with hot yellow as the glare of our lamps lit it, but unmistakable. 'My God!' cried I. 'What?' said Hotchkiss. 'Nothing!' I answered, and the moment passed.

"'I've made a great sacrifice,' I told the whip as I got in. 'They all have,' he said, and hurried by.

"I do not see how I could have done otherwise then. And the next occasion was as I rushed to my father's bedside to bid that stern old man farewell. Then, too, the claims of life were imperative. But the third time was different; it happened a week ago. It fills me with hot remorse to recall it. I was with Gurker and Ralphs—it's no secret now, you know, that I've had my talk with Gurker. We had been dining at Frobisher's, and the talk had become intimate between us. The question of my place in the reconstructed Ministry lay always just over the boundary of the discussion. Yes—yes. That's all settled. It needn't be talked about yet, but there's no reason to keep a secret from you. . . . Yes—thanks ! thanks ! But let me tell you my story.

"Then, on that night things were very much in the air. My position was a very delicate one. I was keenly anxious to get some definite word from Gurker, but was hampered by Ralphs' presence. I was using the best power of my brain to keep that light and careless talk not too obviously directed to the point that concerned me. I had to. Ralphs' behaviour since has more than justified my caution. . . . Ralphs, I knew, would leave us beyond the Kensington High Street, and then I could surprise Gurker by a sudden frankness. One has sometimes to resort to these little devices. . . . And then it was that in the margin of my field of vision I became aware once more of the white wall, the green door before us down the road.

"We passed it talking. I passed it. I can still see the shadow of Gurker's marked profile, his opera hat tilted forward over his prominent nose, the many folds of his neck wrap going before my shadow and Ralphs' as we sauntered past.

"I passed within twenty inches of the door. 'If I say good-night to them, and go in,' I asked myself, 'what will happen ?' And I was all a-tingle for that word with Gurker.

"I could not answer that question in the tangle of my other problems. 'They will think me mad,' I thought. 'And suppose I vanish now !—Amazing disappearance of a prominent politician ! ' That weighed with me. A thousand inconceivably petty worldlinesses weighed with me in that crisis."

Then he turned on me with a sorrowful smile, and, speaking slowly, "Here I am ! " he said.

"Here I am ! " he repeated, "and my chance has gone

from me. Three times in one year the door has been offered me—the door that goes into peace, into delight, into a beauty beyond dreaming, a kindness no man on earth can know. And I have rejected it, Redmond, and it has gone——"

"How do you know?"

"I know. I know. I am left now to work it out, to stick to the tasks that held me so strongly when my moments came. You say I have success—this vulgar, tawdry, irksome, envied thing. I have it." He had a walnut in his big hand. "If that was my success," he said, and crushed it, and held it out for me to see.

"Let me tell you something, Redmond. This loss is destroying me. For two months, for ten weeks nearly now, I have done no work at all, except the most necessary and urgent duties. My soul is full of inappeasable regrets. At nights—when it is less likely I shall be recognised—I go out. I wander. Yes. I wonder what people would think of that if they knew. A Cabinet Minister, the responsible head of that most vital of all departments, wandering alone —grieving—sometimes near audibly lamenting—for a door, for a garden!"

4

I can see now his rather pallid face, and the unfamiliar sombre fire that had come into his eyes. I see him very vividly to-night. I sit recalling his words, his tones, and last evening's *Westminster Gazette* still lies on my sofa, containing the notice of his death. At lunch to-day the club was busy with his death. We talked of nothing else.

They found his body very early yesterday morning in a deep excavation near East Kensington Station. It is one of two shafts that have been made in connection with an extension of the railway southward. It is protected from the intrusion of the public by a hoarding upon the high road, in which a small doorway has been cut for the convenience of some of the workmen who live in that direction. The doorway was left unfastened through a misunderstanding between two gangers, and through it he made his way. . . .

My mind is darkened with questions and riddles.

It would seem he walked all the way from the House that night—he has frequently walked home during the past Session—and so it is I figure his dark form coming along the late and empty streets, wrapped up, intent. And then did the pale electric lights near the station cheat the rough planking into a semblance of white? Did that fatal unfastened door awaken some memory?

Was there after all, ever any green door in the wall at all?

I do not know. I have told his story as he told it to me. There are times when I believe that Wallace was no more than the victim of the coincidence between a rare but not unprecedented type of hallucination and a careless trap, but that indeed is not my profoundest belief. You may think me superstitious, if you will, and foolish ; but, indeed, I am more than half convinced that he had, in truth, an abnormal gift, and a sense, something—I know not what—that in the guise of wall and door offered him an outlet, a secret and peculiar passage of escape into another and altogether more beautiful world. At any rate, you will say, it betrayed him in the end. But did it betray him? There you touch the inmost mystery of these dreamers, these men of vision and the imagination. We see our world fair and common, the hoarding and the pit. By our day-light standard he walked out of security into darkness, danger, and death.

But did he see like that?

Fontana Books

Fontana is best known as one of the leading paperback publishers of popular fiction and non-fiction. It also includes an outstanding, and expanding section of books on history, natural history, religion and social sciences.

Most of the fiction authors need no introduction. They include Agatha Christie, Hammond Innes, Alistair MacLean, Catherine Gaskin, Victoria Holt and Lucy Walker. Desmond Bagley and Maureen Peters are among the relative newcomers.

The non-fiction list features a superb collection of animal books by such favourites as Gerald Durrell and Joy Adamson.

All Fontana books are available at your bookshop or newsagent; or can be ordered direct. Just fill in the form below and list the titles you want.

FONTANA BOOKS, Cash Sales Department, P.O. Box 4, Godalming, Surrey, GU7, 1JY. Please send purchase price plus 7p postage per book by cheque, postal or money order. No currency.

NAME (Block letters)

ADDRESS